Blast from the Past

Mary Jane Owen

Pepperback Press

One

A salty projectile flew past my ear as I turned the wheel sharply to the right. With over a decade's experience I stomped on my instinctive response and calmly called to the back of the car, "Cut that out if you want to live."

Giggles and another french fry erupted from the back seat as my daughter and her best friend laughed in the face of my—acknowledgedly mellow—wrath. I plucked the next flying fry from the air and popped it into my mouth as I pulled into a parking spot.

"Are you guys waiting out here or coming in with me?" I asked as I grabbed a folder from the passenger seat. A frantic scramble was my only response and the two hoodlums fell in behind me as I made my way across the small parking lot to the front entrance of the bank.

Pushing my wavy brown hair behind my ear, I smiled over my shoulder at my not-so-mini me. Already well over five feet tall at only thirteen years old, my daughter Kit was built, sadly, just like her mother. Another amazon princess in the making. Her best friend Char was all leg suddenly this year but still several inches shorter than Kit. Both definitely had the potential to be super annoying at times, but were really good kids. I was fairly sure they wouldn't embarrass me in public.

My smile was still in place as I nodded at the potbellied guard at the front door and made my way through the small foyer and into the bank. A row of teller windows stood along the left wall and glass-walled offices along the right. Straight ahead was a small square seating area and a large TV anchored to the wall looping ads for savings accounts and mortgages. I recognized the woman standing at the tiny front desk by sight and knew she would remember my name.

"Hi, Mrs. Welsh! How are you today?" She didn't disappoint.

"Very well, thank you. I need to have a document notarized. Can you help me with that?" I asked, gesturing with the folder in my hand. Was her name Maria? It was definitely an M...

The lady whose name I couldn't quite recall opened her mouth to answer as a hoarse shout ripped through the interior of the bank.

I threw out my left arm, forcing the girls behind me and toward the other woman as I placed myself between all three of them and the source of that very bad sound. My forebrain had not yet identified exactly what was going on, but the back of my brain already knew that it did not bode well for any of us.

I took several steps backwards, pushing the girls toward the glass offices and took in the scene unfolding at the entrance. The security guard was on his knees, bent over with his head almost touching the floor. His hat had fallen off and the bald spot on the top of his head was a stark contrast against the ring of dark hair encircling his head. A man stood over him wearing sunglasses and a bandana over the bottom half of his face. Another man in similar gear was walking toward the line of tellers, yelling at the people in line.

I didn't catch what the second man was saying, but everyone on that side of the bank was moving away from him, toward the back wall. As the man swung his body to the right I caught a glimpse of the automatic rifle cradled in his arms. Glancing back toward the first man still standing over the guard, I noted a handgun in his right hand, which he was using to hit the guard in the back of the head. The guard splayed out flat on the floor and didn't move.

I spared a glance back at the girls. Kit and Char were both pale, eyes big. Maria—Mara?—looked fairly calm. Her back was nearly to the door of the glass office behind her. I motioned her back and herded the girls in behind her. The man at the door was focused on the commotion at the left side of the bank and ignoring us for the moment. I turned to Kit and with a hand on her shoulder, motioned for her to squat down behind the desk, sending Char after her. Maria followed suit without any coaching from me. She was about my age but small like Char.

The three of them fit behind the desk well. I crouched at the end of the desk, trying to keep both men in sight.

"Move! Move!" was all I could make out from the barrage of yelled orders. The man with the rifle was herding the customers into the seating area in the center of the room. Two women and two men, one much older, huddled on the floor amongst the club chairs and square ottomans. The older man was getting awkwardly to his knees.

The man by the door shifted his attention to the group huddled in the middle of the bank and I caught sight of a third bandana-covered man behind him, standing in the foyer and looking toward the exterior doors. The man with the rifle moved toward the tellers, now congregated behind the last window in the row. From somewhere on his person he produced a large bag that he threw over the window to one of the tellers. After more yelling, she began filling the bag with money.

I took note of the jackets both men inside the building were wearing. They each had on well-worn work khakis and thick-soled work shoes. The man in the foyer appeared to be wearing faded jeans and a similar style zippered jacket. Like the first man, he carried a semi-automatic handgun. All three men seemed comfortable with their weapons.

Glancing toward Kit, I found her staring at me intently. I reached over and we grasped hands. When I pulled away she put her arm around Char, who was crying silently with her hand over her mouth. Maria crouched behind them, a hand on the desk to balance herself. We made eye contact and she held her finger to her mouth. I nodded and turned back to the scene unfolding before us.

My eyes were on the man still screaming at the teller when movement near the door caught my attention. The guard on the floor had come to and was trying to gather his arms under himself. The small room was filled with the hoarse screams of the man with the rifle and the crying of the customers clustered on the floor across from the door. The sound of the first man's gun going off cut through all of the noise and echoed into the stunned silence. The guard's body slumped back down to the floor and lay still. The man standing over him was frozen in position, one arm extended down toward his body, gun still pointed at his back.

The moment of silence hung in the air. I allowed myself a slow blink and calculated the options. This wasn't an experienced crew. This was a bunch of gun nuts who were way too comfortable using their weapons. Professional thieves didn't make a mess. They got their money and got out. These men were definitely making a mess. They were unpredictable and that made them dangerous. My initial instinct had been to hunker down and ride this out. But now?

Time for Plan B.

"You stupid son of a bitch!" The gunman on the far side of the room roared at his partner as he swung his gaze—and his weapon—toward the door. The cluster of bank employees behind the counter, no longer under the rifleman's gaze, dropped down as one behind the counter.

The first man, still standing over the fallen guard, screeched, "Watch them!" and gestured with his gun toward the teller area, which now appeared empty. Spinning back around, the rifleman bellowed in rage and sprayed the teller counter in bullets from left to right. Bits of wood and plastic flew like confetti into the air.

Now.

I rose and glided out of the office, pulling the door closed behind me.

Keeping one eye on the armed man in the foyer, who stared dumbfounded at the chaos erupting on the left side of the room, I stepped up behind the first gunman. My right hand closed like a vise on his neck and my left snaked around his body to grab his gun as he lost consciousness. I used my grip on his neck to lean his body back against my chest and keep him upright as I spun us both around to face the foyer.

I spared a split-second's thought for the trajectory of the bullets the gunman at the counter was firing. They seemed to be above waist height so there was a good chance everyone taking cover on the other side would be safe. But my top priority now was the man in the foyer.

My dance partner and I were turning as one toward the foyer, putting his unconscious body between me and his associate. He stepped toward the glass door, one hand out to push. Meeting resistance, he threw his shoulder into the door, gun pointed up at an angle. If he had fired through the glass--or simply realized that he needed to *pull* to open the door—I might have been in trouble. As it was, I had plenty of time to raise my stolen weapon and fire. The door shattered into a million pieces and my target dropped his gun and grabbed his arm, stumbling back and falling against the exterior door.

I didn't wait to watch him slide down to the floor. The sound of the glass door shattering was not subtle. By the time I had turned myself and my unwitting human shield toward the rifleman, he had turned his firing weapon in our direction. I felt the body in my arms shudder with impacts and a line of fire arched across my left bicep.

There was no time for finesse. A million thoughts rushed through the back of my mind but my finger was already squeezing the trigger. I could have thrown the gunman I was holding toward the shooter and ducked behind the concierge desk to my right...but that would have moved the weapon in the direction of the office where my daughter was hiding. I considered and discarded various options, but in the end the part of my brain that runs on instinct—and always had, no matter how much training or conditioning I'd been through—was calling the shots. The back of my brain decided in that split second that the danger this man represented to my child was unacceptable.

I watched his body fall to the floor as the rest of my brain caught up and connected the neat bullet hole in the man's forehead to the echo of the recoil in my hand.

Dismissing the man on the floor in front of the counter as no longer a threat, I dropped my human shield and spun to the gunman in the lobby. He was still down. I allowed myself to relax a little as I walked over and scooped up his weapon. I thumbed on the safety and stuck the gun in the waistband of my pants. The would-be robber was crying and rolling around in the pieces of shattered glass, clutching his arm. I spotted several zip tie style handcuffs attached to his belt. I grabbed them and flipped the man onto his stomach. He screamed like a girl as I wrenched his arms behind him and tied them together, his face grinding into the glass littering the foyer.

Hopping up, I went to the body I'd abandoned by the concierge desk. Crouching down beside him I placed my fingers gently on his neck and waited a second. There was a faint pulse, so I rolled him over and applied a zip tie to his hands. He was completely limp and easy to manhandle into position.

The third gunman was going to be a problem; dead bodies always were. I knew what I'd find but I still crouched down beside him and felt for a pulse. I pulled his bandana down to reveal his face. It didn't spark any recognition. This guy wasn't here for me.

I stood and walked to the glass wall of offices. The woman—Maria--peeked over the desk, her eyes wide with fright. I pushed open the door and walked quickly around the desk. Kit was crouched behind the desk chair, fingers wrapped around it like she was considering jumping up and hurtling the chair through the glass wall at any moment. Her friend Char was sitting on the floor behind her, arms wrapped around her legs and her face buried in her knees.

"Mom!" Kit cried when she saw me. She pushed the desk chair away and leapt to her feet. Stumbling around Maria, Kit threw herself into my arms. I felt the last of my adrenaline drain away and I pulled her back down to the floor, burying my face in her hair. Char came shuffling over on all fours a minute later and I raised an arm to let her join our hugfest.

Behind Char, Maria crossed herself and bowed her head. When she looked up I extended my right hand and she caught it with her left, squeezing. Suddenly her eyes went wide.

"You're bleeding," she said blankly, then her eyes rolled up in her head and she slid to the ground.

The girls and I broke apart and fussed over her until the paramedics arrived. Maria was starting to come around but I insisted they take her first. Within minutes another team was there, ushering us out to the waiting ambulance.

As we walked through the lobby of the bank, a pair of suited detectives wandered the scene, taking notes. The man by the concierge desk had already been removed, so presumably he was still alive. The rifleman by the counter was still there, now covered with a sheet.

We walked through the shattered glass wall into the foyer, where the final gunman was sitting against the wall, clutching his arm to his chest under the close supervision of two uniforms. He glanced up as we walked past. His eyes got wide and he shrank back against the wall.

In the parking lot there were two ambulances pulled to the side and another one arrived as we crossed to meet them. Maria was sitting on a stretcher beside one and she perked up when she saw us, waving. We were escorted to the next vehicle where I was directed to hop up on a stretcher and the sleeve of my shirt was cut open.

"It's just a scratch. Can you just clean it and wrap it so we can go home?" I asked the paramedic.

"Umm...this looks like you were grazed by a bullet, ma'am." the young man stuttered out. We lived in a nice neighborhood and he acted like he'd never seen a bullet wound before. *Must be new* , I thought.

"Regardless, it isn't deep and doesn't even really need stitches. This has all been fairly traumatic and I'd really just like to get the kids home."

A firm voice spoke from behind me and the paramedic cast a relieved look over my shoulder.

"We need to get your statement before you can leave, Mrs..."

I turned to see one of the suited detectives rounding the stretcher, looking at me expectantly. This was the older of the two men from inside the building. He was barrel-chested and solidly built despite his age. I didn't doubt he'd played football in high school 30 years ago.

"Welsh." I replied flatly. My chances of getting out of this without a paper trail had just disappeared. I'd known they were slight to begin with, but it was still a disappointment.

Things are about to get complicated .

"Mrs. Welsh," the detective echoed. "We have a well-ventilated wannabe bank robber who says he was shot by wonder woman. You wouldn't happen to know anything about that, would you?"

I burst out laughing. "Well, someone got the good drugs today, didn't they?"

The detective lifted an eyebrow at me and I shrugged.

Still smiling, I turned to the girls. The sight of them clinging to each other beside the stretcher killed my amusement. I considered and discarded several options, then said, "Char, call your mom and have her come pick you guys up, okay? I may be stuck here for a little while but you guys don't need to be. Lead with the fact that you're okay so she doesn't freak out." I winked at the girls and got small smiles in return. Kit held my gaze a little longer, then turned to watch Char make her call.

I turned back to the detective as the paramedic finally started cleaning my arm.

"How can I help you, detective...?" I asked calmly. I knew as soon as they reviewed the video from the bank the questions would escalate but I was fairly certain I'd be cleared without too many hoops to jump through. I just needed to keep them from digging in the wrong direction.

The detective matched my tone. "James. Did you shoot the bad men, Mrs. Welsh?" he asked.

"Yes, sir," I responded.

The detective pulled out his notebook again and began taking notes. He peppered me with questions and I responded slowly and carefully, spelling words when needed. "Full name and address? Date of birth? Employer? Spouse?"

"I'm not married," I corrected.

"You didn't correct me when I called you Mrs. Welsh," the detective made the statement into a question.

"No, it's often easier not to."

"What is your relationship to those girls?" he asked.

Damn, I thought. I was hoping Kit would be picked up by Char's mom before he realized she was mine. "The taller one is my daughter. The other girl is her friend."

"What happened to your daughter's father?" he asked.

Under normal circumstances I'd tell him to fuck off. "She doesn't have one. She was conceived via artificial insemination."

"Hmm," he hummed as he made a notation. I wondered if it said *feminazi*, or something slightly more enlightened. "And do you own a firearm, Mrs. Welsh?"

"Yes, sir," I responded. The number one rule of dealing with lawyers and law enforcement: don't volunteer anything.

"How many?" the detective asked, looking up from his notebook to meet my gaze.

I held his eyes, my face relaxed but not blinking.

"One," I responded, conveying the lie without a flinch. *The only one you'll ever know about.*

"What kind?"

"I own a glock." Totally true statement.

"And where is that gun now, Mrs. Welsh," the detective asked, still staring at my face.

I allowed my lips to curl slightly up at one corner. "It had damn well better be in the gun safe in my bedroom."

The detective nodded and finally looked down and made a notation in his notebook.

Behind him, Char's mother Mallory pulled up at the curb on the road. She jumped out of her car and ran across the well-manicured grass, eyes wild. Her face changed as she recognized her daughter and I spared a brief prayer for the uniform who was running to intercept her. She neatly ducked around him with the grace of a woman who had been attending yoga classes three days a week for at least thirteen years. He never stood a chance.

Mallory careened into the girls, who were still clutching each other next to my stretcher, wrapping both of them tightly as her eyes latched onto my torn and bloody sleeve.

I held up a hand.

"I'm fine. It's literally just a scratch," I announced preemptively. "The paramedic is almost done patching me up." I turned back to the detective, raising one brow. "I assume you need to ask me some more questions?"

"Yes, ma'am," he confirmed.

Turning back to Mallory, I asked, "Can you take Kit with you and I'll pick her up as soon as I'm done?"

Mallory looked like she wanted to pull me into the hugfest but she contented herself with reaching out her left hand in my direction. I met her with my right and she squeezed, her eyes tearing up. "Everyone's fine," I told her firmly.

"Well, not everyone..." the detective pointed out.

I turned to meet his gaze. "The guard...?" I asked, already knowing the answer.

The detective shook his head. I closed my eyes and turned my head away. Mallory, who was still clutching my right hand, used it to pull me to her, nearly yanking me off the stretcher. She dragged the children with her as she forced the four of us into a hug, finally releasing my hand to sling her arm around my shoulder, thankfully high enough not to ruin the paramedic's handiwork.

The girls and I suffered through a long moment and then all three of us began setting boundaries and reclaiming our personal space.

I smiled indulgently at Mallory. "I swear I'm okay, Mal. Get the kids out of here. They need pizza, ice cream, and a fuzzy blanket."

Mallory looked at the girls and back to me, obviously torn between wanting to comfort the children and not wanting to leave me alone. Eventually her mother's instinct won out and within minutes I was watching her bundle the girls into her car and whisk them away. I felt a flash of anxiety that Kit was moving away from me, and I allowed the emotion to surface to my face. I didn't try to hide the shudder that rocked my shoulders or the tears that came to my eyes. Turning my face and raising my hand as if to shield my eyes, I made sure the detective got the full effect of the show.

Two

John

Detective John James left Anne Welsh in the interrogation room and moved back toward his desk. His partner Rob was returning from the other direction and they both dropped into their chairs, looking at each other across the face-to-face desks in silence for a moment. John dragged his hand through his silver hair as Rob shrugged.

"I have no idea what's going on. How about you?" Rob asked.

"Yeah, I got nothing. Did the video come through yet?" John responded, logging into his computer. "Here it is," he answered his own question.

Rob jumped up and rounded the desks to hover over his partner's shoulder as John clicked on the bank's video feed. Four views of the bank's lobby filled the screen in black and white. The view in the upper right corner showed the back of the tellers and had a clear shot of the main entrance. The detectives watched Anne Welsh walk through the doors, the tall brunette smiling.

"Wow," Rob said.

John nodded. Even in the small, gray video, the woman was striking. She was wearing a long sleeve, v-neck shirt that tucked into her jeans, accentuating her surprisingly narrow waist. John had noted, in an entirely professional capacity, that Welsh was a beautiful woman.

In the video the first gunman appeared in the doorway. John kept his eyes on Welsh. He saw her sweep the kids and one of the bank employees into one of the offices and he lost sight of her. Glancing at the other views, he could see her crouched by the side of a desk. There was no sign of the others so he assumed they were hidden behind the desk.

"Damn," Rob said, and John switched his view to the main lobby of the bank where the guard was being executed by one of the gunmen. John backed the video up a couple of seconds and kept his eyes on Welsh. He saw her expression change when the guard was killed.

"Did you see that?" John gestured to the screen.

"See what?" Rob asked, leaning in closer.

John backed up the video again and hit play, pointing to Welsh. "Watch her face when the guard is shot." They both stared at the screen intently. John paused the video again, turning to Rob. "What does that remind you of?"

"A cop," Rob responded without hesitation, "or a soldier. She's dropping into the zone."

John nodded in agreement and hit play again. They watched in fascination as Welsh floated up behind the gunman and spun him around. Glancing at the other views, John swore under his breath and backed the video up again. As it replayed the previous seconds, he focused on the top left screen where the man at the teller desk was spraying it with bullets. He could see the bank employees crouched behind the desk, huddled together, and knew from his time at the scene that there were no bullet wounds, although plenty of small injuries from the flying pieces of wood.

"Look at that," Rob said, leaning over John's shoulder to stop the video. He gestured to another view and John saw Welsh standing with her back to the teller's counter and the soon-to-be dead man with the automatic rifle. She had her hand on the neck of the gunman standing before her. "Look at perp two's face," Rob continued, "he's completely unconscious."

John bent in closer and indeed, the man's eyes were closed and his face slack. John realized he wasn't standing in front of Welsh--he was actually leaning back against her.

"Did amazon soccer mom just vulcan neck pinch this guy?" Rob asked in awe.

John started the video again and they watched the scene play out. In seconds all three men were down.

Once the video stopped, Rob went back to his seat and the two detectives sat across from each other in silence. John pulled up Anne Welsh's record and went through it again. He'd glanced earlier but now he went through every resource available to him.

"There's no law enforcement experience, military service. Nothing to indicate any type of training," he told his partner. "She has one handgun registered and she took a safety course before she bought it. None of this adds up."

Rob shook his head. "CIA? This has to be a cover."

John nodded. "That makes sense. But usually if we ping an undercover profile we get black suits knocking on our door in less than an hour. So far nothing."

"So should we ask? You could send a discrete inquiry to that guy we worked with on the Ortega case. What was his name? Stowe?"

John opened his top desk drawer and began rifling through the cards scattered inside. "Yeah, I think that's right. I've got his card in here somewhere...here it is!" John surfaced from the drawer triumphant, a plain white and blue business card in his hand. "Special Agent Jay Stowe, FBI."

***

Jay

Jay sat at his desk, staring in shock at the black and gray, grainy video still on his screen. His hand was stuck in his thick caramel colored hair, caught halfway through sweeping it up off his forehead while he'd checked through his mail.

The email from John James hadn't rang any bells at first. Then he'd read the detective's note and remembered the case they'd consulted on. Jay was always happy to help the local PD. Since he'd transferred to DC he'd had more opportunities to work with the local departments than ever before in his career—especially the Fairfax, Virginia and Montgomery County, Maryland departments, since they were so closely intertwined with the Federal agencies.

Jay clicked on the image. He zoomed in, knowing his initial thought had to be wrong. The woman on the screen looked so familiar, but he was sure once he got a closer look the resemblance would fade. It didn't. Jay hovered his mouse pointer over the other attachments on the email, premonition making his stomach tight.

The second attachment on Detective James' email was a full page ID sheet with a driver's license pic in the upper right corner. Jay glanced at the data. Anne Welsh, 40. One child, no husband. Address just outside of DC in Fairfax, about 10 miles away from where he sat right now. His mind spinning,

Jay bounced from data point to data point, but his gaze kept coming back to the picture.

Focusing on the problem at hand, Jay put a lid on his churning emotions. He'd taken off his suit jacket when he sat down and as he hunched over his keyboard, his shoulders strained against the white of his dress shirt. As a senior Special Agent he had access to more resources than Detective James. Within minutes he had amassed an impressive amount of data on Ms. Anne Welsh.

Or, at least, on the woman calling herself Anne Welsh. Her cover was excellent but Jay had been in the business of building excellent covers himself, and he recognized the work of another professional. Whether he admitted it to himself or not...he was pretty sure he recognized Anne Welsh.

Standing abruptly, Jay grabbed his suit jacket from the back of his chair and swung out of his office. This late in the day the hallways were almost completely empty. He encountered one other agent in the elevator and shared a silent nod. One of the things Jay liked about his current office was the complete and utter lack of camaraderie or any kind of social community. The nation's capital sucked the office culture right out of people, apparently.

Since leaving the CIA over a decade ago, Jay had bounced through several agencies before landing in the FBI. Since becoming a Fed he'd been assigned to offices in Washington state that sounded (and smelled) like a Starbucks, a unit in Texas with more hats and twangs than a John Wayne movie, and the foreign land of Boston where they apparently spoke a dialect of English that he was completely unfamiliar with.

Finally landing here in DC after successfully closing a particular gory case had been a relief. No office happy hours, no weekend BBQs. The agents in the DC office barely knew each other's names, and that's exactly how Jay liked it.

There'd been a time when he'd socialized with other agents outside of work. In fact, he'd done more than socialize with one particular agent—an agent who looked a whole lot like one Ms. Anne Welsh of Fairfax, Virginia. Her name had been Beatrix...Beatrix Bigotti, but she preferred to be called Trixie.

Jay entered the parking garage and walked to his black government-issue sedan. The person he was then would have judged his current life harshly. He had lived for adventure and was lucky enough to be able to parlay the skills he'd learned as a Navy Seal into a position with the CIA. There he'd found the perfect combination of adventure and intellectual challenge to keep himself satisfied. Just like now, Jay had preferred to work alone, but somehow he kept running into Trixie Bigotti.

Pulling out of the garage, Jay recalled the first time he'd met Trixie. He'd walked into one of her operations without a clue and she'd almost shot him. Honestly, she would have been completely justified in shooting him. Whatever had made her hesitate that day, he'd never seen her hesitate ever again.

It had been hot as hell that day in Baghdad as he'd followed a lead for hours through the more dangerous parts of the city.

Just past nightfall, he'd swept aside an embroidered curtain and ducked into a small market stall and froze.

A tall figure in traditional robes was standing over two dead bodies. Jay reached for his weapon but before his hand could even make contact with his firearm, he was looking down the barrel of a glock. His eyes shot up and he felt the floor drop out from under him. He was about to be killed by the most beautiful woman he'd ever seen. Her hair was covered but her eyes were large and tilted at the corners, her lips full and lush.

A part of Jay was not upset that her face would be the last thing he'd see. But instead of shooting him, she asked, "Who the hell are you?"

The American accent lit a spark of hope and in a split second Jay was all in. "Jay Stowe, CIA."

"Fuck," was her response, but his hope wasn't dashed. "Grab the fat one's feet," she said, slipping her weapon somewhere under her robes and turning to bend over the other body.

Jay rushed to do her bidding and together they moved the bodies to a trunk in the back of the tent.

"I'm Trixie," she said. "You looking for Bahwa Alam, Hot Stuff?"

"How the hell could you possibly know that?" Jay asked, hesitating as he folded the dead man in half.

Trixie laughed like a crazy person and Jay fell a little bit in love with her.

After Trixie helped him bag his target in Baghdad, they'd run into each other again in Ireland. She'd come out of nowhere to save his ass in a warehouse shootout gone bad.

Jay had taken out the last member of the cell—or so he thought—and was standing from his position behind a large wooden shipping crate, when a shot rang out behind him. Spinning, he saw a black clad figure crumpling to the ground...and walking from the shadows was a tall, svelte form he recognized immediately.

Before her face even entered the light, Jay knew it was Trixie and said her name. That slightly crazy laugh rang through the empty warehouse like a bell.

"You're welcome, Hot Stuff," she said as she walked past him, letting her shoulder brush his. "Come help me search the office."

After that they were assigned on a mission together. They went in as a couple to a large wedding. It had been surreal and Jay had given up trying to keep his head on straight. They'd danced for hours, then gone back to their room. The big, soft bed had not been wasted.

Sinking his hands into Trixies curls, Jay leaned down and took her smiling lips and gave her his heart.

The next day Jay held Trixie's hand during the wedding then made small talk with a beautiful French woman at the reception...while Trixie slipped a clear, odorless, tasteless liquid into her husband's drink. They stayed at the party long enough to see the man clutch his chest and fall dead at his wife's feet, then returned to their room to pick up where they'd left off.

When Jay and Trixie landed the next day at JFK, he turned to her expectantly only to find her walking away.

"Trixie!" he called without thinking. Pride wasn't even a factor at that moment.

She didn't hesitate, turning back to smile over her shoulder.

"See you around, Hot Stuff," she called, and disappeared into the crowd.

Jay stood there. Part of him wanted to chase after her, but he knew she was already gone. Picking his heart back up off the floor, Jay put it away and made his way back to his apartment alone. It was nearly six months until he saw Trixie again at CIA headquarters, and that's when everything fell apart.

Flashing his ID at the gate, Jay pulled up to the very same building. It had been over a decade since he'd left the CIA, but he still had contacts here who could tell him about Anne Welsh—and quiet the voice screaming in the back of his head.

Walking into the building, Jay had to sign in, even with his FBI badge in hand. After running the gauntlet he hit the elevator and within minutes was knocking on a closed door. Muffled cursing echoed from within so he knew Bobby was inside.

"Who is it?" came the curt response.

"It's Jay. Unlock the door, man." A second later the door popped open and Jay slid inside, closing it behind him.

The room was huge for an office in a federal building, but every wall and surface was covered in electrical equipment. Seated in the middle of the metal and plastic web was a gamer's wet dream. A cradle chair hung below an array of screens. The main screen was huge and curved, centered in a cluster of slightly smaller monitors, each one displaying either a video feed or data stream of some sort.

"Hey, Bobby," Jay greeted the dark-skinned man who ruled this electronic kingdom. Jay was a big guy, but Bobby—on the rare occasions Jay had actually seen him out of his cradle and standing up—was even bigger. In addition to a couple of inches of height, Bobby also probably outweighed Jay by at least 100lbs of pure muscle.

"Jay, Jay, Jay...hmm," Bobby mumbled to himself. "Let's see what brings you to my little cave on this fine day..." Bobby's fingers flew over his keyboard and within seconds Jay saw his search history pop up on Bobby's main screen.

"The FBI has very politely requested that you not hack their systems."

Bobby ignored him and Jay saw Anne Welsh's driver's license photo pop up on one of the secondary monitors.

"And who is this beauty?" Bobby asked the room in general.

"That's—"

"Hush, you. That was a rhetorical question." Within minutes Bobby had the bank video and easily three times as much data as Jay had been able to pull up about Welsh.

Jay stood and watched the process in fascination. Bobby had been the first person Jay met when he joined the CIA nearly 20 years ago and he never failed to impress. Pulling a chair up,

Jay parked himself where he could see Bobby's screens but not disturb the master at work.

Finally, Bobby hit a key and pulled a thumb drive from the dock at his elbow. He tossed the drive at Jay and raised his arms to lace his fingers behind his head. As Jay snagged the drive from midair and tucked it into his pocket, Bobby swung his chair around to face Jay, his expression alarmingly bland.

"Well, well, well," Bobby drawled.

"It's a cover, right?" Jay asked.

"Of course it's a cover," Bobby replied. "The question is...who's cover?"

"Not CIA?"

"Nope," Bobby confirmed. "Although it does look like it, doesn't it?"

"Can you pull up the record for a deceased agent?" Jay hesitated a moment and said, "Beatrix Bigotti."

The last time Jay had heard that name in this building was nearly thirteen years ago. The moment Jay had walked into the seventh floor conference room and seen her face, he'd known something was wrong.

His handler had given him the heads up that Trixie would be at the meeting, so he'd had a couple of days to prepare himself mentally. Jay was determined to play it cool and be professional. If she wasn't interested in pursuing a relationship, he wasn't going to let his emotions get in the way of completing the mission. Then he'd seen the dark shadows under her eyes, the collarbones protruding from the neckline of her oversized sweater, and his good intentions had flown out the window.

As soon as the briefing was over, Jay had walked over to Trixie's side. She was rising from her chair and he put a hand on her arm to keep her from making a run for it. They stood frozen until the room cleared.

"Join me for coffee?" he asked. He knew better than to try to get her to talk in CIA headquarters.

Trixie looked up at him for a moment, the gears turning behind her eyes. Jay made himself wait for her response while his every instinct screamed at him to pick her up and run away.

"Wow," Bobby said, pulling Jay into the present. Bobby had turned his chair back to his array and pulled up the pic from Trixie's archived file and was maneuvering it alongside the photo of Anne Welsh into his facial recognition program.

The application aligned the two photos and eliminated differences caused by the equipment and lighting of the original photographs. Lines appeared across the two faces, delineating the bone structure under the skin. Calculations appeared on an adjacent monitor defining distances between features, length, depth. The views zoomed in on the left eye in each photo and markers appeared over each color variation.

The machine chirped.

"Wow," Bobby said again.

Three

Trixie

"Detective James, do you intend to charge me with a crime?" I asked calmly. I knew James had suspicions but I also knew my cover was excellent. There was nothing that he could prove.

"What crime do you think I should charge you with, Ms. Welsh?" He flipped the question back at me. The detective had definitely been around the block a few times.

"I shot two men, Detective," I said, pointing out the obvious.

The two of us sat and stared at each other in a rather boring game of chicken. Finally, the detective sighed.

"And there is clear evidence that both of these shootings were in self-defense," James admitted. "The DA does not intend to file any changes against you at this time, Ms. Welsh, but please don't leave town. We may have more questions as we continue our investigation."

"Of course, Detective." I kept my face carefully blank as James rose to his feet.

"Right this way, Ms. Welsh."

I followed Detective James through the warren of hallways and ADA violations until we reached the main lobby. Turning to the detective, I extended my hand and said, "Thank you. Feel free to call me at any time if I can be of help."

I turned back toward the revolving door and slipped out into the late afternoon light. Once on the other side I pulled out my phone to arrange an uber, walking toward the nearest intersection. Fifteen minutes later I was sliding behind the wheel of my own car in the parking lot of the bank. I started the engine and rolled down the windows to air out the car while I texted Kit that I was on my way. I was ripping my torn sleeve off of my shirt when her trademark thumbs up appeared on my screen, which I have come to understand means, "I acknowledge your communication but I have no response at this time."

Glancing at the bank as I pulled away, I could see the shattered glass doors had already been covered in plywood. I wondered briefly if they'd try to get the blood out of the carpet or just replace it.

I made a right turn onto the street, away from the commercial center and back into the neighborhood. A couple of minutes later I passed our house and continued to the end of the street and made a left onto Mallory and Char's street. I pulled my car behind Mallory's in the driveway. Leaving the engine running I threw open the door and got one foot on the pavement when a strident voice rang out from the front porch of the house.

"Turn the engine off, woman."

Crap.

Mallory stood in her front door, hands on her hips, flanked by two extremely judgemental Great Danes. I obviously wasn't going to be able to grab my kid and go. I meekly turned the key in the ignition and grabbed my phone, exiting the vehicle at a more sedate pace.

"Yes, ma'am," I said as I walked up the driveway, appropriately chastised.

On the porch Mallory pulled me in for a tight hug and I patted her on the back awkwardly while the dogs leaned into the back of my legs. Our other friend Diane popped out of the house behind her and swept up both of us.

"Oh my god, Annie!" she cried as she tried to smoosh Mallory and me into a single human.

"I'm okay, Diane. I swear." I finally pulled back from the hug and reached down to pat the dogs' heads. "How are the girls?"

"They're okay," Mallory answered. "They didn't really see anything. The news is saying three people dead. The guard and two of the bank robbers. *What happened?*"

Mallory and Diane pulled me into the house and Kit came running down the stairs and launched into my chest. I braced myself at the last moment so we didn't go tumbling back out the door and down the porch stairs.

"I'm okay," I repeated, stroking my hand over her hair, playing with the peek-a-boo blue streak in the wavy dark brown strands.

We stood there for a moment, her arms tight around me, while I tried to project calmness back to her. Sliding my hands down to her back I squeezed her to me and pressed my cheek against the top of her head.

"We're both okay, baby." I held the squeeze for one more moment and then pulled back to look at her face.

At thirteen, I was starting to see the woman Katerina would become. She was going to be tall and strong and beautiful. Actually, she was already all of those things and I was so proud of her.

"You did good today, baby." I pulled her back in for a quick hug and anchored my arm across her shoulders to maneuver her around the dogs.

Char was standing behind Kit and I reached out and pulled her into a one-armed hug.

"You *both* did great today. Thank you," I told the girls sincerely as we moved through the dog bed-strewn living room to the kitchen table.

Mallory pulled out a chair at the end of the table. "Sit," she said firmly. I noticed her first aid kit was already on the table.

"Mal, it really was just a scratch. The paramedic did a great job cleaning it and bandaging it."

"Please let Mal check you out, Annie. We've all been worried sick," Diane said quietly as she settled into a chair.

I sighed and sat. Mallory carefully removed the paramedic's perfectly fine bandage and replaced it with a much more sophisticated version, topped with pink vetwrap. Having a veterinarian for a neighbor had come in handy on more than one occasion and this was not the first time I'd been adorned in the brightly colored bandages designed for patients with four legs.

"Happy?" I asked them both, smiling.

"Not in the slightest," Mal replied, her expression grim as she sat in the chair beside me. "Having my daughter and her best friend and my best friend caught in a shootout has pretty much ruined my day."

Looking at her face, I could see the tension around her eyes and noticed for the first time how pale she was.

"I'm sorry. The girls were never in danger, I swear."

Mallory squinted at me. "And you?"

I barked out a laugh. Oh, she really does know me too well.

"Maybe just a teeny, tiny bit." I smiled, but Mallory was having none of it.

"What happened?" she asked again and I sighed. I'd known there was no way I was getting out of this.

"What did the girls tell you…" I trailed off as Kit and Char joined us at the table.

"We just heard a lot of shouting, and then gunshots. We couldn't really see anything," Kit said. She looked at me searchingly and I sighed again, finally giving in.

"Someone started yelling and when I looked there was a man wearing a mask, holding a gun on the security guard. The three of us and one of the ladies who works at the bank hid in one of the offices—"

"Yeah, I got that," Mallory interrupted. "Now get to the part where you leave the safety of the office to confront the men with guns."

Mallory's expression was grim, Diane's face was drawn, and Kit looked upset and confused. Char looked like she was on the verge of tears again.

I took a deep breath and tried to speak in an even, calm tone. "One of the men shot the security guard and one of the others started screaming at him. The situation was out of control. *They were out of control,*" I emphasized. "I was afraid they'd just start shooting up the place and a lot of people were going to get hurt." I met Kit's intent gaze. "I made a split second decision to intervene. I'm sorry if I scared you, baby."

"I was just so worried about you. The shots were so loud and you just moved toward them and I couldn't see what was happening," Kit told me, her voice cracking. I could see the tears in her eyes, but they didn't fall. I reached out my hand and she met me more than halfway, pulling my hand to her and resting her forehead against it.

"Oh, baby. I'm so sorry."

Kit raised her head and looked me in the eye. "I don't want you to be sorry. I want you to promise me that you'll never move toward the sound of gunfire *EVER AGAIN.*"

"Umm..." I tried very hard to never lie to my kid and to always think about promises before I made them. This was a hard one.

I tried to see it from Kit and Mallory's perspective. To them, my behavior seemed incredibly reckless.

"A long time ago, before you were born," I started, mind racing to edit my words as they came out, "I had some specialized training. I know it seemed like I was taking a huge risk, but I swear that wasn't the case." I looked around the table, seeing everyone's confusion.

"Remember when we did the gun safety course?" I asked Kit. "Do you remember how I hit the bullseye every time and the instructor was kind of impressed?"

Kit nodded.

"You never told us that," Mallory said in surprise, glancing at Diane for confirmation. "You told us about the class but not that you'd hit every bullseye."

"I didn't want to make a big deal about it." I turned back to Kit. "But I actually have a lot of experience with guns. I know this was a scary situation, but I have training and I swear I knew what I was doing." I was still holding her hand and I gave it a squeeze. "I'm sorry I left you and you were worried about me."

Kit's face relaxed and the anger faded away. She dropped her head to our hands again and I reached over and rubbed my other hand across her shoulders. I looked over at Mallory helplessly, taken aback by her squinted eyes. *Oh crap*, I thought. *There's a dog with a bone.* As if summoned by my bad metaphor, one of Mallory's dogs chose that moment to stick her head into my lap.

"Hi, Rosie," I smiled down at the extraordinarily large head trying to wedge itself between me and the table. Rosie was a beautiful warm golden red—hence the name—with black masking around her mouth and eyes. I was pretty sure there weren't a whole lot of brain cells behind those big brown eyes, but what Rosie might lack in intelligence she more than made up for in personality.

"Poor Rosie, I know you have no idea what's going on. You're upset because we're upset," I told her in a sing-song voice. "You're a good girl, Rosie. Everything is okay." I loved the short, soft hairs between her eyes and rubbed her there as she sighed into my lap.

"Rosie would have made a wonderful therapy dog," Mallory said, "If she weren't so clumsy."

I couldn't contain a giggle. "Oh man, I can just imagine all 200lbs of her trying to maneuver around a hospital room." Rosie abandoned me for Kit, her other favorite person. My daughter released my hand to grab the dog's big head and plant a kiss on her nose.

"Hey, girls," Mallory said, "Rosie and Roscoe need to go out. Why don't you take them into the backyard and play ball with them for a little while. They've been slugs all day."

Kit and Char were hustling out the patio doors with the two big dogs a moment later and I girded my loins to face yet another interrogation today. Detective James had nothing on Mal and Diane.

"Yes, dear?" I said preemptively, smiling sweetly at my best friend.

Mallory narrowed her eyes at me and I listened wistfully to the girls playing with the dogs outside and wished I was with them.

"You have *training*?" she asked. "Since when? From where? You've never mentioned this before. And why didn't I know you were some kind of sharpshooter?"

"There's obviously a lot more going on here. Spill," Diane said firmly.

"I've told you that I had to drop out of college after my parents died, right?"

Mallory nodded. "For a year..."

"Yeah. After some false starts I ended up doing some part-time work with an organization that paid my tuition and also provided some rather unorthodox training. It was weird, but I enjoyed it." *That's putting it mildly.* "Until I didn't."

"What kind of company pays for college and self-defense training?" Diane asked slowly. I could see her wheels turning.

Mallory leaned closer, her eyes huge, and scream-whispered, "Were you a call girl?"

I burst out laughing. "Oh my god, no," I finally got out. "I was working for the government." I couldn't decide if Mallory's expression was relief or disappointment. Maybe a little bit of both.

The patio door slid open and a herd of elephants rampaged into the room. Or maybe it was just 400lbs of dog and two teenage girls. Either way, the conversation was—thankful-ly—over.

It took us another ten minutes or so to work our way out the door, but soon Kit and I were climbing into our car and heading back down the street. Turning the last corner I felt nearly giddy with relief to see the pale yellow facade of our 1940s rancher. Kit hit the garage button and by the time I pulled into the driveway the door was all the way up and I pulled right into the cool, dim interior. The door closed behind us and we sat there for a moment.

I released my seatbelt and turned toward her, examining her downcast profile. It had been a long day for both of us. Reaching out, I swept her chocolate waves behind her ear, revealing her peek-a-boo blue streak.

"You okay, baby?" I asked quietly.

Kit nodded, then turned and threw herself into my arms, sobbing against my shoulder. I held her, twisted awkwardly in the seat, the emergency break digging into my side. I held on tight, one hand stroking her hair, while she cried out all of her fear and anger and thirteen-year-old hormones.

***

Jay

Jay pulled into the precinct parking lot and slid his dark sedan in among the patrol cars. Stepping out of the revolving door he asked the desk sergeant for directions and soon found himself standing beside a pair of desks set face to face.

"John?" Jay said.

The detective jumped then smiled in recognition and stood up to hold out his hand. "Jay! Sorry, I was a million miles away. You got my email?"

Shaking the older man's hand, Jay returned the smile. "I did," he confirmed. "And I am intrigued."

"Aren't we all?" John said, sitting back in his chair.

Two hours later it was getting dark as Jay was walking out of the precinct, a second thumbdrive in his pocket. This one held the recording of James' interview with Anne Welsh. Opening the door of his sedan and sliding behind the wheel, he turned on the ignition and sat with the door open, considering his options. His instincts were screaming at him to go to Welsh's home address and confront her.

Two things were holding him back. First, there was the slim chance that he was wrong. The last few hours had kindled a hope in his heart. He felt as if he was waking up from a 13 year fog. It was terrifying how much he wanted this woman to be Trixie. But that was the other side of the coin. What if it was true? If Trixie had been alive all of these years and never reached out to him. A fist squeezed around his heart at the thought.

Jay stamped down his emotions and headed back into DC. He'd review everything he had collected and sleep on it. He needed to get his head on straight before he confronted his past.

Four

Trixie

Forty sucks , I thought, rolling out of bed. After emptying my bladder, I stuck my head in Kit's room. Her night light was cycling through the colors of the rainbow, making the outline of her body visible. I stood in her doorway for a moment, listening to the sound of my daughter breathing.

I made my way back to my bedroom and checked the time. Only half an hour to dawn, so there was no point in trying to sleep again. There was a time when I'd trained myself to sleep no matter the time of day. When you're on a mission, you take the opportunity to rest when you can. But those days were long gone and I'd reverted back to my natural state. If the sun was up, so was I.

Pushing my pillows against the headboard of my bed, I leaned back and replayed the previous day. I'd spent the first couple of years after Kit was born religiously dedicated to regaining then keeping my edge. I'd developed a routine I could do in my basement and drove out to the middle of nowhere for target practice on a regular basis. I'd maintained peak fitness and was on alert 24/7. But as the years had gone by, I'd relaxed that vigilance. At the five year mark I decided to breathe a little, and then again at the 10 year mark I'd relaxed my vigilance even more. Who could possibly still care about Trixie Bigotti after all of these years? I'd gone from a 27-year-old in the peak of her physical prowess to a 40-year-old single mom who no one would look at twice.

Over the years, the illusion has gradually started to become the reality. I'm not pretending to be a soccer mom. I *am* a soccer mom. I have a kid. That kid plays soccer. And I freaking love it. Watching my kid annihilate the other team is one of the greatest pleasures of my life.

I still do my workout routine every morning and I still go target shooting every couple of months...but I also hit the drive thru on the way to soccer practice and grab a frothy coffee on my way back to the house after dropping Kit off at school. I've allowed myself to enjoy this life I built for my daughter. It is, after all, my life too.

Then, yesterday, I had needed all of those skills from my old life. In the moment there wasn't a second's hesitation or doubt. I trusted that I would reach for those skills and they would be there. And they were. But now, in the last few minutes before dawn, I allowed the anxiety of the what-ifs to wash over me and sent a thank you out to the universe that my confidence hadn't been misplaced.

Shaking off my mood, I picked up my phone to pull up my schedule for the day. I had a 3pm call with my publisher but otherwise Kit and I were free. My deadline was weeks away and school was a distant June memory. Today we definitely deserved to eat lunch out.

I was considering restaurant options when my nerves started to tingle. I froze and let my mind drift for a moment, trying to pinpoint the source of my sudden spike in adrenaline. There was nothing. No sound at all. And that was the problem. The finches that perched in the tree beside my bedroom window had stopped their morning chatter.

Someone was in my yard.

I rolled to the side and allowed my body to slide from the bed and silently dropped to the floor. Reaching under the bed I angled my arm up to pull out the gun safe I'd built into the bottom of the boxspring. Setting it on the floor in front of me, I entered the combination and flipped open the lid to pull out the small handgun inside. I slapped one of the clips into the gun and shoved it into the deep pocket of my leggings. The other two clips went into the opposite pocket.

Sliding the box back under the bed, I reached for my phone. Checking that it was on silent, I slipped on my shoes and moved silently into the hallway and toward Kit's bedroom.

Crouched beside her bed, I reached out a hand to touch her face. "Wake up, baby," I whispered. In the summer I often wake Kit up like this, so I'm not afraid she'll scream. She does her usual sleepy stretch and slowly opens her eyes. When I know she's looking at me, I put my finger to my lips, then lean in close, kneeling by her bed. "I think someone is trying to break into the house. Put your shoes on," I whispered in her ear. Kit jerked her head back and stared at me. I handed her the shoes sitting beside her bed. Like usual, she'd been sleeping in a t-shirt and pj shorts.

While Kit slipped on her shoes I grabbed the bra hanging over the back of her desk chair and passed it to her. My tank top had built-in support, which is plenty for me, but my kid needs something more robust if we're going to be running for our lives. I moved back to the door, staying low, and listened intently. There it was, a squeak. From the kitchen, I thought. Every door in the house squeaked obnoxiously, except for one. Likewise, there were only a handful of floorboards that were properly nailed down.

I'm the only one who can move through this house quietly.

Kit came up behind me and I turned back to her, once again placing my finger before my lips. I stepped out onto the third floorboard of the hallway and pointed to it, motioning again for silence and walking my fingers down the plank, and pointing to the door to the guest bathroom at the end of the hall. Kit's eyes flared in comprehension and then narrowed at my sneakiness. This will definitely be another awkward conversation.

I led the way down the hall quickly, Kit right on my tail and staying on the quiet floorboard. The door to the bathroom opened silently and we slipped inside. Knowing no light would leak through the specially treated mirrored glass in the window or below the custom fitted door, I flicked on the switch. Kit was only a couple of months old when I bought this house. I placed her in her bouncy chair and sat her outside the bathroom door for safety and ripped this room down to the studs. I rebuilt it using the same fixtures and the same style tiles, but with a couple of extras.

In addition to the one way bulletproof glass and the layer of panels that make the room soundproof, bulletproof, and imperceptible to infrared cameras, I also added a secret compartment in the back of the medicine cabinet. I opened that cabinet now and pressed on one of the innocuous white screw covers along the top edge. The shelves swung forward to reveal a space built into the void between this room and the kitchen, with a door on the other side accessible from the ceiling of the pantry. The contents of this space had changed over the years. Today they held two black backpacks. I took them both out and handed one to Kit.

"This room is soundproof," I told her in a normal tone of voice. "I know you have questions, but right now we just need to get out of the house, okay?"

Kit nodded. She'd put the backpack on and her knuckles were white where she gripped the straps, but her face was calm and she met my gaze, waiting for directions. *That's my kid.*

"We're going to climb onto the porch roof and go through the back of the yard to the Mr. and Mrs. Blume's house," I told her. "And we're going to steal their car. Got it?"

Kit looked at me for a moment, wheels turning. "Sure, Mom. You're either completely insane or this is the end of the world. Either way it should be fun," she said. "Let's go."

"Excellent." I switched off the light and opened the window over the toilet slowly. Stepping up onto the seat, I placed my other foot on the tank and stepped out of the window onto the porch roof. Turning back to the window, Kit was right behind me.

We made our way carefully to the edge of the roof where a reinforced trellis provided the perfect ladder down to the screened area where our AC unit sat. Hopefully whoever was in my kitchen didn't have friends watching the backyard, but even if they did, the strategically placed trees and bushes should give us enough cover to get to the fence.

The moment Kit's feet hit the grass, I grabbed her hand and we sprinted to the back of the yard. I grabbed a small section of fence and easily lifted it free of the rails, slipping through the gap. Kit followed me and I replaced the boards. We were now in our rear neighbor's yard. They knew me enough to wave when we were both out mowing, but I knew them much better.

Joe and Susan Blume were both retired and had lived in this house for 30 years. They rarely moved before 11am and had a well-maintained blue hybrid minivan that they hardly ever pulled into their garage, which was full of Joe's "projects".

Kit and I walked quickly along the tall cedars that edged the Blumes' yard, and paused at the corner of the garage. I walked quickly to the passenger door of the car, hearing it click open as it recognized the duplicate fob in my bag. I opened it and slid into the seat and across to the driver side, Kit slipping into the seat behind me. I pressed the ignition and the electric engine flared silently to life. The only noise was the quiet grind of the tires against the pavement as we pulled from the driveway and backed into the street. Putting the car into drive, we headed west, toward the mountains.

***

Issac

Issac Es finished his sweep of the house and braced himself as he contacted his employer.

"Report," the curt voice demanded.

"The house is empty, sir," Issac said succinctly. "We know they were both here ten minutes ago, but something must have tipped the target off and they slipped away."

Issac braced himself for an explosion. The silence that followed was much, much worse.

Pulling the phone away from his ear, Issac confirmed that the line was still active. He focused on controlling his breathing and mentally began counting. Issac lived a dangerous life. Approaching middle age, he was quite old for a man in his profession. One of his greatest assets was his ability to understand the powerful men he worked for.

"What is your next step, Mr. Es?" asked the voice on the other end of the call.

...38. Issac stopped his count and responded promptly. "I have men canvassing the neighborhood and the e-team has put tags on all of her accounts. They are now installing worms in every camera in a two mile radius and will be running facial recognition patterns in real time on all of the streams." Issac made sure he ended firmly. He'd done all he could do.

"Very well, Mr. Es. Carry on."

Click.

Issac once again checked his phone, this time confirming that the call had disconnected. He placed his phone back in his pocket and took a deep, calming breath. The rewards were high, but so were the risks.

***

Trixie

Maneuvering around the steering wheel, I wiggled out of my leggings and into a comfortable pair of stretchy mom jeans. The park was deserted this time of day and we were well hidden in this little corner, but I still kept an eye on our surroundings. Pulling the gun and clips from my discarded leggings I slipped them into my generous pockets and tucked the leggings back into my bag. Behind me Kit was changing in the back seat. I'd packed a plain gray tee and black cargo pants for her. I didn't have to upgrade the clothes in her bag as often these days as I'd done once, but I still checked every six months or so.

"All good?" I met her eyes in the rearview mirror.

"Yeah," Kit answered, flopping back on the seat and brushing her hair out of her face.

"Yes..?" I prompted.

"Yes," Kit said firmly. "Yes, you can now tell me what *exactly* is going on."

I sighed, dreading this conversation. I'd made the best decisions I could at the time, but it was easy to see other options with hindsight.

Kit shimmied through the opening between the front seats and settled into the passenger seat beside me. She sat there looking at me expectantly and I had no one to blame but myself. I'd taught the child to be confident and inquisitive and now it was biting me in the ass.

"I don't really know where to start," I admitted, angling myself in my seat to face her.

"Start at the beginning," she replied logically, mimicking my position.

"I'm not really sure where that is," I told her honestly, looking down at my hands.

"Okay...," Kit drawled. "What's the biggest lie you've told me."

My eyes flashed up to meet hers in surprise.

"My real name is Beatrix," I told her softly. "Beatrix Bigotti. Everyone always called me Trixie."

Kit took in a deep breath through her nose, lips pressed together. Her eyes glistened with tears before she pressed them shut and I braced myself for an eruption.

Her lashes swept up and she met my gaze. "Hi, Trixie. Nice to meet you."

Suddenly we were both crying and hugging each other awkwardly across the center console of our stolen minivan.

"Thank you, baby," I told her between sniffles. "I wanted to tell you so many times, but I just didn't know where to start." I shook my head, pulling back into my seat but keeping hold of her hands.

"What happened to Trixie, Mom?" Kit asked.

"Trixie died. She was killed in a warehouse fire in Baltimore thirteen years ago," I began, digging through the center console to find a relatively clean napkin to wipe my nose. "But her troubles started a lot earlier.

"Everything I've told you about my childhood and my parents was true. Except for one small detail. Nothing my family did was legal. The laundromat, my dad's club, the restaurant my grandfather's friend ran that we used to eat at every Friday—"

"The place with the lobsters?" Kit asked.

"Yeah, the surf and turf. I loved that restaurant. We'd sit in the big round booth in the corner and they'd bring out the lobster that my grandfather had picked out for me. I felt like a princess." I laughed, rolling my eyes.

"When I was a kid I never thought anything of the brown paper bags full of money that were always changing hands. I was twelve before I realized that normal families didn't have a bookie who stopped by the house once a week."

My smile faded as memories began to crowd in. I'd been such a daddy's girl. Finding out that my hero had feet of clay had been hard enough. The fights that resulted when I began to question the way things were had torn our family apart.

"When I finally realized what was going on, I didn't handle it as well as I could have." I frowned, remembering. "There were some spectacular fights and we all said things we shouldn't have."

I looked at Kit again, "But I want you to know, my parents weren't bad people and they really loved me. I've had a long time to think about things since then. They were in a situation that they could only see from the inside and that they had no way to get out of. They'd both grown up in that life and they didn't know anything else."

I shook my head. "In the end, they let me go." I balled up the abused napkin and tossed it into the back seat. "One of the counselors at my school told me about early admission, and I went for it. I forged my dad's signature and applied to UCLA in my junior year. And I got in. I packed my bags and left one morning before they were awake. I left a note. That was it." Regrets made my eyes start to water again, but I took a deep breath, determined to get through this story.

"I loved college. I started writing letters to my dad. I knew he was mad—and hurt and betrayed—but I was still daddy's girl. I think my mom was more insulted than anything, as if I thought their life wasn't good enough for me. I didn't know how to make her understand." I broke off and stared out at the dense trees around the parking lot for a moment. I'd given this a lot of thought over the years.

"Of course, the problem was that she wasn't completely wrong. I looked at their life and I did judge it. Even with what little I knew then, I could see the money laundering and tax evasion. Years later I learned the business was even worse than that." Kit didn't need to know everything, so I left it at that.

"My dad and I were so much alike. Everyone used to tease us. He never responded to any of my letters, but when I got my tuition bill for the second semester, it was paid. And every semester after that." My eyes started to water again and I had to stop for a moment. Kit reached out and grabbed my hand again.

"Then I got a bill that wasn't paid and I didn't know what to think. I went back and forth. I was driving myself crazy. Finally, I tried to call and didn't get an answer, which was odd. I let it go another couple of days. Then I tried to call the main number at the Laundromat." I shook my head and stared through the window.

"I didn't know the person who answered, but they told me that both of my parents had been killed in a fire. The house, everything was gone. They were gone. They'd been gone for months and I hadn't had a clue."

I was all cried out and I just sat there, holding my daughter's hand.

"Did you go back?" Kit asked softly.

I shook my head. "There was nothing to go back to. Everything was gone. I'd even missed their funeral."

"Your grandparents?"

"My Nana had already passed before I left. I tried to call my grandfather but I got my Uncle Cal and he told me the old man didn't want to talk to me and cursed me out." I frowned, remembering my frustration.

"There should have been some money, at least from the house, the insurance, whatever. I tried calling my dad's lawyer but he wouldn't talk to me. He told me Cal was handling everything and I knew that was a deadend. I just got the runaround and I had to give up. I had to get a job to pay my tuition bill and drop my class load but my heart wasn't in it. At the end of the semester, I ended up withdrawing."

"This is when you got the job with the *special training*?" Kit raised her eyebrows at me.

"No, not yet. I got a job on campus. I actually had a couple of jobs on campus. But then I was offered that job, and I accepted." I paused.

"And that job was..." Kit prompted.

"Well, it was more that I was recruited, than offered a job," I stalled.

"Recruited by whom?" she inquired archly.

I sighed. "Well...the CIA, of course."

Five

<hr>

Jay

Jay spotted Detective James standing in front of the Welsh house as he pulled up. Dawn was breaking over the treetops and there were uniforms canvassing the neighborhood on both sides of the street. Leaving his sedan by the curb, Jay slammed out of the car and tried to smooth the tension from his face as the detective strode over to meet him.

"Thanks for the heads up, John." Jay extended his hand. The detective shook it briefly before taking his hand back to run it through his hair. It looked like he'd been doing quite a bit of that already this morning.

"It wasn't completely altruistic. I'm hoping you can shed some light on this mess," James admitted, gesturing to the house behind him.

"You said there was a break-in?" Jay prompted.

"Oh, it's much more complicated than that," the detective scoffed. "One of the neighbors apparently has the entire block under surveillance. We'll be discussing privacy laws with them at a later date, but for the moment we're more concerned with the army of black clad men they tracked through this house in the early hours of the morning. At least a dozen, each with automatic weapons and tactical equipment."

The detective shook his head in wonder. "It looked like someone was taking down a third world dictator in the middle of suburbia. This was definitely a professional operation, but according to what we're seeing, they left empty-handed."

"And Anne Welsh was the target?" Jay asked.

"It certainly looks that way," James confirmed. "Can you think of any reason there might be a professional hit out on our Ms. Welsh?"

"I don't have a clue," Jay admitted. "If my suspicions are correct, then Welsh is a cover. I've just started going through the intel we've collected" Jay grimaced, "That was my project for this morning."

"Sorry to call you so early, but I figured you'd want in," James shrugged.

"Yeah, you figured right," Jay agreed.

The two men began walking toward the house. At the porch they were met by the second detective on his way out.

"Jay, this is my partner, Rob Hanson," James introduced the two men, who exchanged handshakes.

"I'm on my way to the station," Rob told them. "We have access to the cloud account for Mrs. Kravitz and the team is going to start going through the footage to try to make some IDs. I'll let you know as soon as we have anything." With a sloppy salute, Hanson bounded off the porch and headed toward one of the cars parked along the curb.

Jay and Detective James continued into the house and paused for a moment in the doorway to take in the carnage. Furniture was overturned and stuffing strewn across the floor. It looked like every cushion had been slashed, every drawer emptied.

Despite the chaos, Jay couldn't help searching for signs of Trixie in the trappings of an ordinary, suburban home. The living room furniture looked like it had been large and comfortable. The remnants of cherry red pillows were thrown over the back of a partially de-stuffed armchair in a yellow floral pattern. In the kitchen the cabinets were clean and white farmhouse style. One door was hanging off its hinge and the rest were thrown open to reveal a few boxes of cereal, pots, and mismatched pieces of tupperware. The rest of the contents, as well as the shattered remnants of many dishes were scattered across the dark-stained hardwood floors.

Walking into the bright and sunny dining room, Jay noted the pretty turned legs on the white table and matching chairs. Each chair had a cushion with a different colorful pattern, all slashed. The rug under the table was a traditional oriental pattern in an unusual palette of pink and purple and orange. Before the devastation the house would have been warm and bright with surprising pops of bright color.

"We're not expecting to get any prints in here," the detective told him. "From the images these guys were all gloved up." Gesturing for Jay to follow him, he said, "The interesting stuff is upstairs."

At the top of the stairs James turned toward the end of the hallway and stepped into the bathroom. The medicine cabinet above the sink was open, showing the empty recess behind it.

"This room is completely reinforced. It's soundproof and bulletproof," the detective said succinctly.

Waving Jay back to the hallway the two men entered the master bedroom. The sun had fully risen and the room was bright and airy, done all in white and shades of cream.

"Take a look at this," James said, dropping to a knee beside a box partially hidden under the bed.

Jay squatted beside him as the detective pulled the box out from under the bed and flipped it open. Inside was a neatly compartmentalized gun box, the weapon missing.

"Hmmm," Jay wondered. "Looks like a very nice toy goes in that spot."

"I agree," said James, bending down to run his arm under the bed. "And check out the niche that this box fits in. Custom made. Again, very nice."

Jay rolled down from his heels to his knees to peer under the bed. The recess was perfectly sized and nearly invisible to anyone not looking for it. When he raised his head, James was looking at him intently.

"I don't know who Anne Welsh is, but she's no amateur." James raised his eyebrows. "Anything you'd like to share, Agent Stowe?"

Jay sighed and moved back to his feet. "I have my suspicions, John, but you've been working this longer than I have. I haven't even had a chance to look at the data you gave me last night." *Or the data from Bobby.* He'd been avoiding looking at Trixie's files, hiding from the memories. And now it looked like she might be in the wind again. Jay was kicking himself.

Wandering around the room, he approached the long dresser under the window. The top was swept clear and a cascade of broken bottles and jars littered the floor. Crouching down alongside the mess, Jay picked up a small picture frame lying face down amidst the rubble. As he flipped it over he shook the broken glass onto the floor and froze.

This wasn't a crappy DMV pic or a grainy security video still. This was a high res picture taken in good lighting of a woman who Jay knew, with absolutely zero doubt, was Trixie Bigotti. And she was standing with her arm around a teenage girl who looked just like her.

Forcing his body into life again, Jay asked in a completely normal voice, "Welsh has a daughter?"

James came up behind him and glanced at the pic over his shoulder. "Yeah. Katerina."

Jay nodded, still frozen inside. "Do you have her DOB in your notes, by any chance?"

"I should." James pulled his notebook from his suit pocket and flipped back a couple of pages. "Here it is. Yup. Just turned thirteen on April 5th."

Jay nodded again, face blank. "Anything else to see up here?"

James shook his head. "No, the girl's room and the guest room are in the same state. We haven't found any other secret hiding spots."

The detective led the way from the master bedroom, pausing in the hall to push open the door to the next room. Jay leaned his head in and took in the teenage girl's bedroom in a glance. The ceiling fan blades were pink, but the curtains were a bright blue velvet. The room was an eclectic mix of little girl and young woman.

As Jay followed the detective down the stairs, he glanced toward the door of the master bedroom, where the empty gun box was visible lying on the floor. He couldn't see the empty picture frame sitting face down on the top of the dresser, but he patted the photo resting in his suit pocket as he walked out of the house.

James continued to talk to him and Jay must have responded in a way that made sense, but his mind was a million miles away.

***

"Join me for coffee?" Jay asked quietly as the briefing began. He'd watched the emotions cross her face intently and he'd been sure she was going to say no.

"Maybe when we get back, Hot Stuff." Jay felt his chest expand with relief. Maybe wasn't *no*, and he'd take it.

"Hey, Trixie, got any experience with kids?" A deep voice interrupted them from the end of the table. Trixie jumped and her face paled.

"Well, teenagers," the senior agent clarified, "which I hear are much, much worse." They all laughed as Trixie's color returned.

"Dear god, no," Trixie deadpanned, causing the room to erupt into laughter again.

When everyone had settled down, the senior agent continued. "For those of you who don't know me yet, I'm Mitch Glass and I'll be the senior agent on this operation." Mitch turned to a whiteboard set up behind him and flipped it to display a series of headshots, interconnected with lines of various colors.

"Drugs are flooding into local schools and we've pinpointed this high school as the epicenter of the traffic. It's time to get in there and shut it down."

***

Trixie

Kit had been quiet since we started driving west and I was getting nervous. She'd taken all of my revelations amazingly well so far and now I was waiting for the other shoe to drop. When I couldn't take her silence any longer, I reached out and turned down the radio.

"Tell me what you're thinking." I was not one to pussyfoot around.

"My sperm donor," Kit replied without hesitation. "Was that all bullcrap?"

I made a conscious decision to ignore the softcore cursing and answered her honestly.

"Mostly, yes." We had turned onto route 15 and I was looking for a good place to switch cars. My eyes were scanning the businesses on either side of the road, but I glanced over at Kit and met her gaze. "Everything I've told you about him is true, but it didn't come from a sperm donor profile."

"Who was he? How did you know him? Were you guys dating?" Kit peppered me with questions that I'd known would be coming for thirteen years but was still somehow unprepared for.

My first instinct was to say that he was someone I worked with, but that didn't sound right. It hadn't been like that and I didn't want Kit to think of it that way.

"He was someone I cared about," I said, "but our timing wasn't right." That felt like the truth.

"Every time I saw him there was a connection, but our work always got in the way. Then suddenly work threw us together.. .and things *progressed...*" I glanced over at my teenage daughter and wiggled my eyebrows and gave her an exaggerated wink, "...if you know what I mean."

"Oh dear god," Kit whispered. "Please, don't. Don't ever do that again."

We both giggled like idiots. I offered to pull over so she could throw up at the thought of her mother having sex and she punched me--not gently--on the arm.

"Aha!" I pointed at the farmer's market up ahead. "There we go!"

I pulled the minivan into the overgrown field used as a parking lot and drove between the haphazard rows until I found a nice--but not too nice--silver sedan. I pulled in a couple of rows over and we walked casually to the sedan. I pulled the handle and it popped open. Kit did the same on her side and we were in. The interior was steamy but I ignored it and leaned under the steering wheel to hotwire the car. Thirty seconds later we were headed back down route 15 the way we'd come.

As we turned back onto route 7 headed west again, I felt Kit turn in her seat to look at me.

"Where are we going?" she asked.

"West Virginia," I answered shortly.

"Who are we running away from? The CIA? Or the Bigottis?"

I laughed. "Probably both, at this point."

"Who were you running away from thirteen years ago?" Kit asked, serious.

I sighed. "The Bigottis," I told her. "Specifically, my uncle."

"The one who yelled at you when your parents died?"

"Yup, that one. At this point he and my grandfather are the only ones left, and my grandfather is in his nineties. And yeah, I'm pretty sure Uncle Cal is the one who put the hit out on me."

"Why?" Kit asked, amazingly calm about all of this.

I wondered briefly if she wasn't processing it or if she thought she was humoring her poor mother's paranoid delusions. Giving a mental shrug, I answered honestly.

"I'm not really sure. I hadn't heard from anyone for years and suddenly Uncle Cal called from out of the blue. I don't even know how he got my number."

"What did he want?"

"He asked me to come to Baltimore to see him. I was in the middle of a big project and I'd just found out about you. I had zero bandwidth for a guy who had cussed me out after my parents died." I frowned, remembering my less than gracious refusal. "I told him to fuck off and hung up."

"Classy, Mom."

I shrugged. "A couple of weeks later two guys tried to grab me while I was walking into my apartment building. It didn't go well for them, of course."

"Did you kill them?" my bloodthirsty child asked.

"No," I replied defensively. Geez, you kill a couple of bank robbers and suddenly you're Dirty Harry. "Actually, they got away and it was totally your fault."

Kit looked at me in surprise, then comprehension hit. "Morning sickness?" she asked apologetically.

"Yes, you horrible child. Morning sickness, afternoon sickness, and evening sickness. 2AM sickness. I had a window from 11 to 11:30 when I could eat food without immediately barfing it up." She may have heard this complaint more than once.

"Sorry!" Kit replied in a sing-song voice, all hint of apology gone.

"Hmm," I frowned at her. Yes, I was definitely one to hold a grudge.

"So two guys tried to grab you and you fought them off and they got away..." Kit prompted.

"At first we all assumed it was something to do with the project I was working on. It was an interagency operation targeting a mafia-funded drug ring. I'd been working as a substitute teacher at a high school in DC—which was insane, by the way. My handler pulled me out and I got shuttled to a short-term assignment out of town." I looked over at Kit accusingly. "Flying did not help the morning sickness."

"Sorry," she said, a bit more contrite this time.

"By the time I got back they'd been able to confirm that there was a hit on me—but it was under my real name. My cover was intact. There'd been no movement on the drug ring so they put me back in the school. The attack seemed to be unrelated, but I was on guard and being careful." I remembered the stress and anxiety of those days, all compounded by the ever present nausea. "Then I ran into an old friend."

Six

Jay

Jay watched Trixie on the monitor as she moved down the sidewalk in front of the school in the grim early morning light, her body completely hidden by her heavy black duffle coat. There were only two days left before the school closed for the holidays and they were running out of time.

There was a direct connection between a Columbian gang and a DC area drug ring that ran right through this high school—they just had to find it. Jay fisted his hands on the console in front of him.

We're so close, he thought.

On the monitor Trixie almost slipped on the icy sidewalk and Jay fought the urge to burst out of the surveillance van and run to her side. Since seeing Trixie again at the previous day's briefing, Jay had been struggling with his instincts. Trixie was a professional and didn't need his protection or his help. And if he got in the way of her doing her job, he knew it would not go well for him.

Outside of the van, the sun was moving higher and students were starting to drift toward the school. They congregated on corners and moved in small packs around the building. Jay noted the members of each grouping, paying close attention to the students their team had already identified as individuals of interest. There was a major supplier here, but they needed to figure out who it was before everyone scattered for two weeks over the holidays.

By the time the bell rang and the streets cleared of students, Jay had drained the coffee from his thermos and was going back through his notes in frustration. They'd cleared all of the teachers and none of the students seemed to be dealing. Their target had to have a direct connection to the drugs coming out of Columbia.

A three-tap knock had him spinning around, gun in his hand and aimed at the back of the van. The door opened slowly.

"Hey, Mitch," Jay greeted the older man, holstering his weapon out of sight. "Trixie is inside, with about a thousand pimply-faced teenagers. Logs are up to date."

"Thanks, Jay," Mitch said, pulling himself into the other chair in the van's interior. "I picked up the last of the background checks," he said, tossing a manilla folder onto the console. "No red flags, unfortunately."

Jay grimaced as he picked up the folder and scanned through the contents. These were the office staff, the secretary, the counselor, etc. The last file was the janitor, John "Butch" Tranetti. He'd transferred in from another school, but he had nearly a dozen years with the district and twenty more as a school janitor in Baltimore. Shaking his head, Jay dropped the file back on the console and spun in his chair.

The bell range faintly in the distance. The interior cameras showed students spilling out into the hallways and chaos reigned for several minutes until, in another mad rush, the process reversed itself. Students poured into classrooms and the hallways emptied out a second before the bell pealed again. The teachers standing at each door turned and walked back into their rooms.

At the top of the far left monitor, Trixie turned and walked back into her assigned room. Her big black coat was gone and Jay could see she was wearing black leggings under a long, loose tunic. The black and white surveillance cameras didn't show much detail, but Jay knew she still had dark circles under her eyes and her cheekbones had progressed from *prominent* to *cuts glass* .

"Stop obsessing," Mitch said, without looking up.

Jay looked at the other agent sharply. "What?" he asked, playing dumb.

"Trixie would not be flattered by your concern," Mitch told him flatly.

"You see it, though, right? Something's wrong?" Jay threw his hands up in frustration. "I know she can handle herself, but obviously something is going on."

"Yeah…and it's none of your business," Mitch told him bluntly. "If Trixie wants your help, she'll ask for it."

Turning to look at Jay, Mitch said firmly, "Focus. That's what Trixie needs from you right now. Help her figure this out before we lose two weeks."

Jay nodded reluctantly and turned back to the video feeds. The exterior of the school was quiet on three sides. Along the rear sidewalk, a single man in a denim jacket was rounding the corner with his hands in his pockets, a duffle bag over his shoulder. Inside, the kids were all still in class so the hallways were nearly empty. A teacher walked down the hall, cradling a bowl of soup and went into an empty classroom to eat their lunch in peace. The janitor was descending the staircase at the rear of the building, holding a broom. All looked normal.

Jay began to reach for the folder of background reports when the last monitor caught his eye. The janitor had reached the ground floor and opened the door leading to the end of the building. From the camera's vantage point, Jay could only see an arm appear through the door holding a duffle bag. The janitor grabbed the bag, the arm disappeared, and he shut and locked the door. He moved quickly back up the stairs, the bag over his shoulder.

"Holy crap," Jay said out loud. "That's it!"

"What?" Mitch asked, "What did you see?"

Jay reached forward and played back the video feed. They both watched the handoff, then Jay moved to the exterior view to show the guy in the denim jacket walking away.

"Damn," Mitch said, "we don't have enough to ID this guy."

"No," Jay agreed, "but we've got the janitor cold."

Mitch agreed. "Yeah, but before we bring him in, let's see what he does with that bag. In the meantime, let's do a deeper dive into his background. We need family, friends, neighbors, etc."

"I'm on it," Jay confirmed, already looking forward to wrapping things up quickly and finally getting the chance to sit down to that cup of coffee with Trixie.

***

Trixie

"A friend from Baltimore?" Kit asked.

I nodded. "A friend of my parents...actually, he was a distant cousin of my dad's, so, technically family."

My stomach knotted as the memories came rushing back. My grandfather would sit at his kitchen table, holding court, and it seemed like people were always coming and going. They'd bring him brown paper bags with strapped bundles of cash, they'd talk and he'd send them back out. I knew there were weekly deliveries that were made or picked up all over town. Some drove down from Philly or up from DC.

I'm not going to lie, I enjoyed the commotion. The coming and going and the laughing at improbable stories. I was the only grandchild, the only girl, and I was the princess. The men would often bring me little gifts. I had a place at that kitchen table and grown men would stand and speak to my grandfather while I sat and did my homework.

I wondered if my grandfather was still alive. I could have looked it up probably, but it was a hornet's nest I wasn't eager to kick.

"Family like...*family*?" Kit asked with air quotes, wagging her eyebrows suggestively.

I laughed at her but nodded. "Yeah, pretty much," I admitted, shrugging. "I had lots of *uncles* who worked for my dad or my grandfather."

"Not *funny* uncles, though, right?" Kit asked, half serious.

"No, dear," I replied, rolling my eyes.

"Okay, then," Kit said with a smile.

"Well, not completely okay," I cautioned. "They may not have been pervs, but they definitely weren't on the up and up, either."

"This is the money laundering part?" she asked. *Nice to know the kid is paying attention.*

"And illegal gambling, counterfeit merchandise, smuggled cigarettes, pretty much every kind of organized criminal activity you can make money off of...except drugs. Or so I thought." My smile was gone now and I frowned as I pulled into a gas station. I left Kit in the car and paid at the window with cash. A couple of minutes later we were back on the highway.

I glanced over at Kit and she was looking at me expectantly, so I sighed and continued my story.

"Turns out that this friend of my dad's, Butch, was the janitor at the school I was working at. I'd seen him in the halls but I hadn't recognized him. It had been so long," I shrugged. "I felt bad for not recognizing him right away."

I'd been in the middle of a sentence when the bell rang and the students leapt from their seats and ran from the room as if chased by the hounds of hell. I sighed, used to the abrupt end to the last period of the day. I'd been substituting at this high school on and off for a couple of months now as the agency worked on the Columbian angle from different directions.

Shuffling my notes back into the folders on the desk, I grabbed my purse from the bottom drawer and pulled my coat from the back of the chair. As I shrugged into the coat my long sweater rested against my baby bump. I'd been lucky so far that my pregnancy was easy to hide. The benefits of a long torso, I guess. Good luck finding a one piece swimsuit that fit, but plenty of room to hide an extra human being.

Ready to walk out the door, I turned back to grab the container of cut veggies sitting on the edge of the desk. It was pretty much untouched and I frowned down at my well-covered belly. "You need to let me eat, kid," I whispered, for the hundredth time. Veggies in hand, I closed up the classroom and made my way down the hall to the teacher's lounge. Placing the container in the small fridge, I vowed to make an effort to eat them the next day.

My mind had drifted to Jay and Mitch out in the surveillance van—and our shared angst about the upcoming deadline imposed by the holiday—when I felt a presence behind me. Turning casually, I found the school's janitor standing in the doorway to the lounge, a rather odd smile on his face.

"You don't remember me, do you?" he said.

I was taken completely off guard. There were a million places he could have recognized me from, and none of them were good.

"It's Uncle Butch, Trixie," was absolutely the last thing I expected him to say. "Your Uncle Cal has been looking for you, honey," was the second to last thing I expected him to say. He could have pulled a gun on me at that minute and I probably wouldn't have moved. My brain was turning over rather slowly, trying to figure out how to handle this situation. Among the issues was the fact that my name wasn't Trixie, as far as anyone in the school was concerned.

Apparently no response was needed. Butch approached, hand outstretched, and I braced myself. But he was only offering a piece of paper. I accepted it carefully, expression still blank.

"Cal would like you to meet him at his warehouse tonight. He'll be there until midnight, if you can stop by." He met my gaze as he stepped back. "Your grandfather is getting old, honey. They'd both like to see you." With that, Butch turned and walked away, leaving me frozen, holding the note from Cal without a clue as to what I was going to do about it.

Making my way out of the school, I turned west and began walking down the still slippery sidewalk. The sky was already gray and the chill cut right through my bones. The ice on the ground sent a chill through my shoes and I wondered briefly if my ankles were swelling. *Classic.*

The unmarked white van pulled up alongside me. Casually scanning my surroundings, I quickly stepped off the curb and hopped in, trying hard not to grunt as I lifted my extra load into the seat. The van took off and I was still pulling the door closed as we rounded the next corner.

"We got him, Trix," Jay called excitedly from the rear of the van, beckoning me to him.

I had to hold onto the door for a moment, my stomach still back on Clinton Street. Mitch looked over in concern but I caught his eye and shook my head. Mitch had been around the block more than twice and I knew I was skating on thin ice there. Swallowing down the bump's opinion on the state of the roads in the city, I swung myself between the gap in the front seats.

"Lay it on me, Hot Stuff," I said as I squeezed past Jay and made my way to the other seat.

***

"—Wait. What? Hot Stuff?? Did you really call that guy *Hot Stuff*?" Kit's exclamation pulled me out of the past and I glanced over at her bug-eyed judgement and quickly glanced away. We'd crossed into West Virginia a while back and were getting close to the cabin I'd prepped for just such an emergency.

"Was this...*Oh. My. God.* This guy Jay is my *dad*!" Kit had her epiphany at two decibels over the legal limit in this county and I glanced in the rearview mirror to see if dogs had started following us.

"Yes, dear. Jay was your sperm donor," I responded calmly. It had no effect.

"My dad's name is a single letter and my mom called him *Hot Stuff*. I think I'm having a panic attack." Kit clutched dramatically at her chest while I stared, narrow-eyed, at the road.

"May I continue?" I asked.

"Yes, please do," Kit responded sedately, content that she'd made her point.

***

I tried hard not to flop into the seat next to Jay. After a long day playing teacher I was ready to put my feet up and veg on the sofa, but now my real work began. I ignored my sore back, swollen ankles, and ever-present nausea and focused on the man next to me. It wasn't a hardship.

Jay was one of the few men who didn't have a problem with my height. He had a couple of inches on me, but I'd found over the years that it didn't matter. Even men my height and taller were often intimidated by a tall woman. From the moment we'd met, Jay had never once stumbled over treating me as an equal—physically or professionally. And that was damn sexy. Add to that a wicked sense of humor and the fact that he was built like a linebacker and the entire package was hard to resist. And for one very naughty weekend, I hadn't.

Looking at Jay sitting in the back of that surveillance van, I could see the shape of his shoulders, big and round with muscle, under his coat. He looked warm and I felt cold through to my bones. But now was not the time. We both had a job to do and I had at least three other complete sets of baggage to get through as well.

While I'd been admiring his shoulders, Jay had leaned forward over the video console and was pulling up clips from earlier in the day. On one screen he showed a man in a denim jacket walking with a duffle bag. On the other screen he showed my new/old friend Butch.

I watched Butch accept the duffle bag and cursed under my breath. Jay turned to me sharply and I had a split second to decide what to share with him.

At this point I was dealing with the emotional and physical ramifications of my unexpected bump, the potential that there was a hit out on me, family drama which may or may not be mafia-related, and now I'd been personally contacted on a private family matter by our prime suspect on a case that we had about 36 hours to blow open before all of the players scattered for three weeks. *Crap.*

I needed help and, conveniently, the person in front of me happened to be smart and capable and one of the few people in the world I felt comfortably trusting with my life. It was time to bend before I broke.

Jay had launched into the background info he'd been able to hobble together so far on Butch and I cut through his speil.

"I know this guy," I said abruptly and he stumbled to a halt mid sentence.

"He's an old family friend. And to make things even more complicated, he approached me today and asked me to come to this address tonight." I pulled the piece of paper Butch had given me and placed it on the console between us.

Jay glanced at the paper and I knew he'd memorized the address in that second, then he glanced toward the front of the van. He looked back at me, eyebrows raised. I shrugged. I'd worked with Mitch before and had no reason not to trust him. Raising my eyebrows I threw Jay's silent question back at him. He nodded firmly and I returned the gesture, decision made.

"Hey, Mitch, we've got an issue," I called up to the front of the van. A second later the van sidled up to the curb and come to a stop. My bump stopped a second later and a wave of relief washed over me. I'd been doing my best to ignore the nausea but riding in the back of the van was really putting my mental fortitude to the test.

The older agent ducked through the opening to the front seats and leaned a hip onto the console.

"What's up?" he asked seriously, his face calm and confident.

"This guy," I gestured at the still frame of Butch on the screen, "made me." I told him. I watched Mitch's muscles around his eyes tense infinitesimally. "I'm pretty sure he works for my Uncle Cal...who is pretty dirty, I think."

Both men in the van just stared at me as if I'd dumped a huge steaming pile of shit into their nice neat operation. Which of course I had. They'd been riding high from finally identifying a strong suspect and my revelations were an unwelcome complication.

"The good news," I told them, "is that this is confirmation that Butch is mostly likely the conduit bringing the drugs in from Columbia. He's got the connections. And while it's not awesome that I may have a family member involved, it's someone I haven't seen since I was in high school. So there's that," I finished weakly.

Mitch sighed and pinched the bridge of his nose.

"Trixie has an address where he's going to be tonight," Jay inserted helpfully.

"Yeah, at least my Uncle Cal will be there. I'm not sure about Butch. Either way I think it's a solid lead." I gestured toward the slip of paper on the console.

Mitch nodded, shaking off his consternation at the change in trajectory and rolling with the new data. "Jay, get as much info as we can on Trixie's Uncle Cal and this address and we'll go scope out the location." Mitch picked up the folder in front of Jay on the console and tossed it lightly into my lap. "Review the background we came up with on this guy Butch and let us know what we missed." With that Mitch ducked back into the front of the van.

I began flipping through the folder, ignoring Jay's eyes on me. The info on Butch was pretty shallow and I grabbed a pen from my purse and began making notes wherever I could. It had been a long time and for most of the known associates I could only remember first names, but it was a start. The van had started moving again and I was breathing slowly and evenly to keep the nausea at bay.

When I finally closed the folder, Jay was pulling a couple of sheets of paper off of the printer.

"Whatcha got?" I asked, keeping my tone casual.

"Ownership history of the warehouse on Bolton," he said, passing me the top sheet. "And this one is known associates of Calvin Dean Bigotti."

I glanced at the warehouse info and sat the paper down on the console, reaching for the second sheet. "This may help me fill in some of the blanks on the info I added to Butch's file." I opened Butch's folder and began crosschecking names, but I could still feel Jay watching me.

Exasperated, I turned to him. "What?" Forcing myself to take a deep breath I pushed down the ever present nausea and lowered my tone. "What's wrong, Jay. Have I suddenly grown another head?" *Because I have.* I tried to smile to take the sting from my words. None of this was his fault. *Except it kind of was.*

It takes two to tango, I reminded myself.

"Trixie, I think you should sit tonight out," Jay said quietly.

"What are you talking about?" I was back to struggling to keep an even tone. Professionals did not scream at their colleagues like fishwives. Or slap them. "Why would I do that?"

Jay sighed and leaned forward in his chair, his face open and earnest.

"I'm worried about you, Trixie." He reached forward and tugged one of my hands toward him and my anger drained away. His fingers were rough as he ran them over my hand, stroking across my knuckles. Memories of a far away location, full of sunlight and warmth and this man were running through my head.

He came a little closer and I imagined the heat from his body reaching across the empty space between us. Then he said, "I can tell you're not at the top of your game and I don't want you to get hurt."

I pulled my hand back, the nascent warmth in my heart from his concern turning into a burning ball of fury.

"My game, Jay," I told him very clearly, "is just fine." My voice was so cold I imagined each word as an icicle stabbing right through those firm, round pecs.

Jay sat back in his chair as if he could feel my imaginary icicles and I realized my nausea was suddenly gone. Nothing like a good old fashioned flash of rage to settle one's stomach, apparently.

"God, Trixie," Jay said, rubbing his hands down his face, "I don't mean it like that. And we both know that even if you were at half speed you'd still be able to kick my ass."

"And don't you forget it, Hot Stuff," I replied, somewhat mollified.

"But please don't lie to me, Trix. I know something's wrong. You don't have to tell me, but I can see it. You've lost weight, you're tired. Even your balance is off." Jay caught my gaze and held it.

"Jay—" I began as the van slowed and rolled to a stop. Mitch popped back through the opening to the cab and the moment was lost.

Swinging into the third chair, Mitch started switching on the screens and setting the cameras into position. We were parked at the other end of the block but the warehouse was clearly visible.

"I drove around the block and there's an exit on the opposite side as well. That one has a large overhead door. Jay, take this remote and set it on the telephone pole on that corner to get us a view."

"On it," Jay said. He took the remote from Mitch and stuffed it in his jacket pocket. Giving me one last look, he slipped through the back door of the van and disappeared into the dusk.

"Trixie—," Mitch started before I cut him off.

"Don't start, Mitch. Unless you happen to have an agent on call who looks exactly like me, there's no one else who can walk into that warehouse right now and get us the information we need. I'm going."

Mitch stared at me for a long moment, and finally nodded. I released the breath I'd been holding and said, "Thank you."

"Don't thank me. Just be careful."

"Always," I smiled.

Behind us the van door opened and we both turned to watch Jay slip back in. A gust of cold air followed him and I could see that the sky had darkened considerably. For a brief indulgent moment I imagined my warm, soft bed, piled high with blankets and pillows. *Not quite yet.*

Seven

Trixie

The sun was high in the sky and Kit was asleep by the time I pulled off of the highway and onto a dirt road almost overtaken with the grasses of summer. I stopped the car and moved quickly to the seemingly random pile of branches lying alongside the track. Unhinging the leg I'd built into the hidden structure I propped it across the path, completely obscuring the turn.

Hopping back into the car I drove us another two miles down the private road until we came to an even more overgrown driveway. The majority of the lots around us housed hunting blinds if anything and even those were seldom used. Still, I was careful as I approached the cabin.

Nestled against the foothills of the mountain, the cabin wasn't visible from the air and was designed to function completely off-grid. I'd stumbled onto it while researching a case and bought it for pennies. The original owner had long since died and since the structure wasn't permitted or easy to find, no one knew it was here. In theory.

"Wake up time, Kitten," I said as I pulled the car under a pine tree. Beside me Kit began to stir.

"Where are we" she asked softly in the quiet left after I'd turned off the engine. Nestled under the tree with thick foliage on two sides, it was like being in a green cave.

"Come on and I'll show you," I told her. We both grabbed our bags and emerged from our pine-cave. I started walking along the edge of a large thorny bush, Kit following in my wake.

"Remember that day you got hit in the head during gym and it took me forever to get to the school?" I asked.

Kit frowned at me. "It wasn't that long," she said.

"It felt like forever to me," I told her. "I was out here. I used to come out here quite a bit while you were in school or at Mallory's house." I ducked under a low-hanging branch and began climbing a small rise. "I haven't been here as often since then. I was so freaked out that day. I was so far away when you needed me."

"Mom, I was totally fine," Kit rolled her eyes at me. "The nurse made way too big a deal about it. I still can't believe they made you take me to the hospital for an MRI. It was dumb."

"Better safe than sorry with a head injury, Babe," I told her. "The nurse totally did the right thing."

"They didn't even do anything," Kit grumbled under her breath.

"Anyway," I cut through her muttering, "this is where I was." Cresting the small rise, I threw out my arms as if I were presenting a palatial estate, when in reality before us was an ivy-covered wall with a half-hidden door.

Kit was noticeably underwhelmed and I couldn't blame her. From the outside there wasn't much to see. That was by design, of course.

I approached the door and swept away the greenery to reveal a hinged panel. Flipping it up I placed my palm on the glass square beneath and the door opened inward with a sigh. Kit followed me as I maneuvered through the half-blocked door and into the dim interior. I pushed the door closed behind her before hitting the light switch. The sound of Kit's gasp was truly satisfying.

We were standing on a balcony overlooking the sunken living area. On one side of the balcony a set of stairs led up to a loft area on the other side of the open space. I turned the other way and took a set of metal stairs down to the living area. At the bottom I looked back to see Kit's head tilted back as she took in the skylight above.

I couldn't help but smile. I was proud of this place and it was nice to finally be sharing it with my daughter, even if it wasn't under the best of circumstances.

"What is this place?" Kit asked, with wonder in her voice. She turned and looked at me. "Did you build this?"

"Not from scratch," I clarified. "I'm good, but I'm not that good."

"Well, it seems slightly more complicated than kitchen cabinets, but at this point nothing would surprise me."

"I'm pretty sure those cabinets are going to be the pinnacle of my DIY legacy." I swept my arm to encompass the interior of the cabin. "The shell was here when I bought the land, but I've retrofitted most of the interior." I led the way into the small kitchen which, not coincidentally, was fitted with the same cabinets as our house.

"I can tell," Kit said, eyeing the kitchen.

"It was easy to order a few extra cabinets when I placed the kitchen order. I just brought them out here a couple at a time in the back of the SUV."

I opened the fridge and tossed a water bottle toward Kit, who caught it midair. On the other side of the kitchen was a small office space with a computer and two large monitors. I sat at the desk and tapped the computer to life. One monitor was divided into multiple small windows, showing exterior views around the cabin.

"We should be safe here for a little while," I told Kit. "Long enough to figure out our next move. No one should be able to tie this property to me and we covered our tracks on the way here."

A booming noise reverberated through the interior of the cabin. Kit and I stared at each other as it took my brain three long seconds to realize that someone was knocking at the door of my super secret hideout.

***

Issac

Issac Es turned the wheel of his black SUV abruptly as he spotted the entrance to the gas station. Weaving between the row of pumps he pulled up next to a matching SUV and lowered the passenger side window. The driver of the other vehicle lowered his window as well.

"Sir, we've positively identified the target. Jacob is inside reviewing the exterior footage."

Issac nodded in acknowledgement and jumped from the SUV. Walking into the shop area of the station, he saw his man exiting the back room.

"Report," Issac barked.

"We're less than an hour behind them, sir. They headed back to the highway."

***

Trixie

"What the hell?" I said reflexively as I stared at the image on the monitor. I grabbed the mouse and zoomed in on the camera mounted outside of the door. *It can't be...*

"Stay here," I told Kit as I pulled the gun from my pocket. Kit sputtered as I closed the office door behind me, palming the panel beside the door to lock it. Taking the stairs two at a time I bounded up to the door and stopped. I started to put the gun away and changed my mind and kept it in my hand. *Crap, this is awkward.*

Flipping up the security stop built into the floor in front of the door, I moved to the side and released the lock and allowed the door to open a crack.

I had good skin and great bone structure and despite the intervening thirteen years, I knew I looked considerably the same. I had a few more curves, but I was definitely recognizable.

Jay was *exactly* the same. Not one gray hair, no little pouch, not a sign of dad bod anywhere. Maybe, possibly, there were a few more smile lines around his eyes...maybe not. *How is that fair?*

We stood there staring at each other, a gun still in my hand.

"Are you going to shoot me, Trix?" he asked. "Or are you going to invite me in and introduce me to my daughter?"

Crap.

"Is that Jay?" an excited voice asked from the level below.

I squeezed my eyes shut for a moment then opened them to nail the man in front of me with a piercing stare. "Funny seeing you here, Hot Stuff. What brings you to this neck of the woods?"

Jay opened his mouth when the voice from below interrupted again.

"Oh. My. God. Did you just call him *Hot Stuff?*"

I did a literal facepalm and took a deep breath, determined to ride out this encounter with some modicum of dignity. I closed the door in Jay's face. Shaking my head at myself, I slipped the gun back into my pocket and disengaged the security lock. When I opened the door again, Jay hadn't moved or changed expression. I stepped back and Jay slipped through without hesitation. Closing the door firmly, I turned to find him standing much too close. He didn't just look the same, he smelled the same too.

"Seriously, what are you doing here?" I asked firmly, putting off introductions as long as possible.

"The car you picked up at the flea market has a GPS tracker on it," Jay revealed.

"That hunk of junk! No way!" I couldn't believe it.

"It's a classic. The owner is in the process of restoring it to its former glory," Jay smiled down at me.

I shook my head. "It's a Toyota Camry. What former glory?" I asked deadpan. "But how did you know I was the one who took it?"

"I didn't," he admitted. "It was a lucky guess. I was crawling through the underbrush collecting ticks and hoping I wasn't about to encounter a bunch of teenagers smoking weed and playing spin the bottle."

"No one does that anymore," interjected the voice from downstairs.

Jay stared into my eyes, all humor drained away.

"Can I meet her?" he asked softly.

I returned his gaze, cycling through emotions and scenarios in my head. "You're not angry?" I asked, equally softly.

"That you gave up your life and career and identity to protect our child?" Jay replied. "No, Trixie, I'm not angry."

He reached out and gently took my hand. "I'm so glad you're alive."

My nerve endings tingled everywhere our skin touched. I pushed down hard on the sensation and tried to think logically. I wasn't a 25-year-old ingenue. I was a 40-year-old single mom trying to navigate a dangerous situation with her teenage daughter in tow.

But I needed help and Jay was the one offering it. Last time that didn't end the way I'd hoped. Maybe this time would be different? Forcing memories away, I led the way down the stairs, where my daughter was *not* waiting in the office as I'd asked.

Making the conscious decision to not spoil Kit's first meeting with Jay by yelling at her for leaving the office, I reached the bottom of the stairs and suddenly realized I was still holding Jay's hand. I felt my face flush as my own child eyed our grasped hands with judgement on her face and I pulled my hand free of Jay's as gracefully as I could.

Kit looked at Jay, at me, and back at Jay. I could see the wheels turning in behind her eyes.

"*Hot Stuff*?" she asked. "Really?"

Choosing the high road, I ignored her. "Kit, this is Jay Stowe." Turning back to Jay, I said, "Jay, this is Katerina."

"My middle name is Leonard," Jay added.

Kit smiled, "That's awful. My middle name is Maria."

"Maria was my dad's mother's name, my Nonna," I told her. They both turned to look at me.

"I didn't know that," Kit said.

"I've had to put a lot of things from my old life away, to keep us safe."

"From what?" Kit asked. "I still don't understand. Was it your Uncle Cal? Is that who you've been running from all this time?"

"It wasn't just Cal," I told her, turning back to Jay.

An alarm rang out from the office. Kit was closest and hurried back into the room.

"Mom, there are guys out by the stolen car," Kit called up.

I arched a brow at Jay. "Friends of yours?"

Jay shook his head and we both hustled down the stairs. One of the screens showed a man in black combat gear uncovering the Toyota. Jay leaned in closer. "I recognize the gear. This guy is part of the group that went through your house this morning. They're led by a mob hitman by the name of Issac Es. Sound familiar? He has massive resources and he's been on your tail all day."

I scanned the camera feeds, trying to size up the opposition. Moving up behind Jay's shoulder, I asked, "How many men?"

"At least a dozen in the immediate area, and twice that on your trail."

"Damn. I really liked this cabin." I muttered.

"The car thing was just dumb luck," Jay assured me. "But Es, he's been canvassing every gas station within five miles of the interstate. You didn't stand a chance." Jay looked down at me, frowning. "Someone wants you bad," he said in concern. "You think it's your uncle?"

I shrugged. "I haven't seen him since that night at the warehouse in Baltimore."

"I need to know what happened that night," Jay said. "But right now we need to get out of here before Es finds my car too. Unless you have another option."

"I thought you knew my mother," Kit said archly. "She *always* has a plan."

Eight

Trixie

The snow had started and I didn't waste time knocking on the door to the warehouse. The knob turned with ease and I pushed inside. The interior was bright, and there were several men moving boxes. They looked up casually as I crossed the threshold. It was as cold inside as it had been outside and I fought to keep my body from shivering. I spotted an office partitioned off to the left and turned that way, closing the door firmly behind me.

The men working in the warehouse went back to their tasks, ignoring me completely as I made my way across the concrete floor. The office had a small glass window set into its door but it was one way glass and I could only see my orange-tinged reflection.

I half expected the door to pop open as I approached, but it stayed closed. I knocked twice and waited for a response from inside. Muffled conversation and the faint scuffs of footfalls whispered through the door. Finally it swung open and a man I didn't know stood there. He was typical beefy mob muscle and I glanced past him dismissively.

Seated behind the desk was my Uncle Cal. He'd aged dramatically since the last time I'd seen him. His hair had gone completely white and his face was gaunt, with dark circles under his eyes.

"How's it going, Uncle Cal?" I asked casually. It passed quickly but I took note of the flash of emotion that crossed Cal's face. It was rage—pure, unadulterated rage. I think I hadn't really believed it until that moment. I hadn't wanted to believe that the hit order had come from my own family. Suddenly, I had no doubt.

By the time Cal rose to come around the desk, the rage was hidden and his face was perfectly blank, but I wouldn't have been surprised if he'd pulled out a gun and shot me on the spot. My entire body tensed and adrenaline pumped through my veins. I spared a thought to my bump, but quickly tamped that down. Our only immediate goal was survival. I'd walked into this warehouse expecting family drama and instead I was face to face with someone who wanted me dead.

"You should have stayed gone, Trixie," Cal said as he crossed the room toward me, Mr. Muscles stepping up behind his shoulder.

"I was planning on it," I told him shortly, preparing to move. I wasn't going to let him get within arm's reach. "You asked me to come here."

"Butch can't keep his mouth shut. Your grandfather knows you're back." Cal moved closer and Muscles reached into his jacket. Any inhibitions I had against interpreting their actions as a threat disappeared.

The split seams on the sides of my winter coat prevented it from being effective against the cold, but they meant that I could kick my Uncle Cal in the face with enough force to send him flying back into Muscles. Sadly the larger man was able to keep his footing, but he had to pull his empty hand from his jacket to keep his boss from falling. I flew through the door, slamming it behind me and sprinted across the warehouse floor back toward the main entrance.

The men working the floor looked up as the sound of the door slamming echoed through the cavernous space but no one moved to cut me off. I was halfway across the floor before someone stepped in front of the door, blocking my exit.

Muscles No. 2 already had his gun out and in his hand.

I skidded to a stop in the middle of the warehouse floor. Glancing back, Muscles No. 1 had exited the office and now had his gun drawn as well.

"Bring her back," Cal called from the office. His voice was hoarse and it sounded like he was speaking through gritted teeth. I was fairly sure that kicking him in the face had not improved his disposition. My instincts were screaming at me to stay out of that office.

"What do you want, Cal?" I called out loudly, hoping he wouldn't shoot me in front of an audience.

Cal was apparently thinking the same thing because his voice called out, "Everybody out! Clear the floor, Gerry."

Gerry was Muscles No. 1. He holstered his weapon back under his jacket and began clapping his hands and ushering the workers from the warehouse floor. I sidled toward the door

"They're not going to help you, Trixie," Cal called, now standing in the office doorway, one hand to his chin. The rage was clear on his face now, the blank mask gone.

As the last of the workers trailed out the door, Muscles No. 2 shut and locked the door behind them, keeping his gun trained on me. Cal was on the move and I swung my head back in his direction, trying to keep everyone in my line of sight.

"Bring her," Cal said, moving toward the second door along the wall. Muscles No. 2 gestured with his gun and began to close the distance between us. I let him. No. 2 was the weak link here. He grabbed my elbow in his left hand and moved me toward the second door. Cal disappeared through the door. Gerry waited and followed us in.

The second half of the warehouse had a large heater set in the middle of the open space with long tables around it where men and women sat naked, sifting powder into small plastic bags. I felt my jaw tense and my face heat. Wanting me dead was one thing. Embroiling my father's business into illegal drugs was another.

"You're disgusting," I told Cal, not bothering to hide the contempt in my voice. "My father never would have agreed to this."

"We do a lot of things your father wouldn't have agreed to these days, Trixie," Cal taunted me.

"Not just drugs, but drugs in schools. Have you no shame?" I knew the answer before I even asked the question.

Cal looked down his nose at me. "For what? Turning a two-bit family business into an empire?" He laughed scornfully. "You're one to talk, little runaway. What rock have you been hiding under, Trixie?"

Cal shook his head, "On second thought, don't tell me. I don't care. I wanted you to see your father's legacy, but it really doesn't matter what you think. You chose to leave this family, Trixie. You should have stayed gone."

Cal waved at Gerry and I spun toward Muscles No. 2, who was still hanging off of my elbow. Using my momentum, I slingshotted No. 2 into the big kerosene heater sitting between the tables.

I glimpsed naked bodies scattering as the heater rocked on its base, but I was already spinning for the door. An explosion erupted from behind me. There was a splash and then screams. I imagined hot oil spraying exposed skin but I couldn't stop. I was already at the door and running full tilt toward the exit.

A shot rang out and chips flew off the concrete wall beside the door to the outside so I veered hard to the right. There was an unused exit on the other side of the building. I needed to find it. I slipped between the tall shelves that lined this side of the building and began running toward the far wall. Halfway down the row there was a gap in the boxes. I slipped through, trading time for cover.

As I was crouched between two boxes, a blast rang out and the entire warehouse shook. The lights went out as the concrete floor tilted up to meet me, the wood crate I rested my hand on sliding forward. For a long moment it seemed like everything was moving in the darkness. My hands and knees met the concrete.

The noise still reverberated through my head, but my eyes were adjusting to the dim light. One hand went to cradle my bump, but we were fine. The shelves had all fallen like dominos and the one I'd been passing through was leaning against the one in front of it. The aisle behind me where I'd been running was full of boxes from the shelf of the previous row and I was hemmed in on all sides.

I sat and listened for a moment. The fire crackled and there were faint creaks and groans as crates and boxes continued to settle, but there were no footsteps or voices.

Cautiously I poked my head up through the tangle of metal shelves and boxes and crates. There was no movement except for the flames licking around the blackened remains of the wall that had separated the packaging room and office. I couldn't see into the room and I spared a thought for the naked men and women who'd been working there. There were no more screams, no cries for help.

Taking a deep breath, I pulled myself through the supports of the tilted shelf, placing my hands carefully on the wooden crate next to me to provide leverage. I was in the middle of a choppy sea of metal, cardboard, and wood. Moving as quickly as I could, I climbed onto the edge of the shelf and began making my way toward the back of the warehouse. I expected shouts or shots at any moment, but I made it to the end of the row without incident. Crouching down on the shelf edge I gripped the twisted vertical support and carefully lowered myself to the floor.

At the end of the rows there were boxes that had tumbled from the shelves and split opened, spilling their contents onto the floor. There were guns. Handguns, rifles, automatic weapons.

What the hell?

My grasp on the enormity of Cal's corruption of the family business exploded. This was so much worse than I ever could have imagined.

On the heels of that thought was the recognition of the danger these weapons might pose if the fire made it to this side of the warehouse. Glancing back over the tumbled shelves I stifled a groan. The fire had worked its way up the far wall and sections of the roof were burning. Above me, the fire raced along the rafters. Time was up. I spun toward the back door and flung myself against it. The door gave slightly. The lever style knob didn't budge, so I backed up and aimed a kick alongside the handle. There was a satisfying thud. I did it again and the door popped open a few inches.

Behind me the roar of the fire was getting louder, punctuated by clatters and bangs. I didn't look back as I pushed my way out of the building and into a wall of falling snow. The light flurries I'd left behind when I entered the building were now a blizzard. The icy surface of the alley behind the warehouse was completely invisible under several inches of snow and it was falling fast. I made my way to the end of the block as quickly as I could on the slick surface. By the time I made it to the corner, the reflection of flashing red lights played against the facade of the adjacent buildings.

Walking quickly in the opposite direction I rounded the next block and worked my way back, circling the neighborhood. My toes were numb in my shoes by the time I made it to where I'd left Jay and Mitch in the van. The van was gone and the street was full of people and emergency vehicles, red lights twinkling in the snow in a bizarre holiday spectacle.

For a moment I stood frozen, wracked by indecision. My family wasn't just "a little dirty". The Bigottis were now running guns and bringing drugs into schools. And I'd just caused the deaths of dozens of people—and millions of dollars worth of merchandise. If Cal and my grandfather had wanted me dead before, I could only imagine how they felt now. If Cal had even survived that initial blast.

Suddenly a huge blast rocked the street as every window in the building blew out. Secondary explosions rang like firecrackers and I knew the flames had finally reached the boxes of weapons. Men in uniforms began pushing the spectators back and roping off the entire block. I drifted away with the crowd.

***

"So," I continued as I stepped over a fallen tree across the path, "to recap, I had a huge bounty on my head that had grown bigger if anything. I had a family that was a major liability professionally as an agent. And I'd caused a fire that no doubt resulted in several deaths as well as millions in property damage...in a building that was likely owned by a family member." I turned back to see if Jay and Kit were suitably impressed by the precariousness of my situation at that point. They seemed to both be paying attention as we traipsed through the undergrowth, so that was good.

"Not to mention the fact that I was nursing a sizable bump that I had grown somewhat emotionally attached to." I side-eyed my child.

"Only somewhat?" she asked on cue, dodging a low hanging branch.

"Remember the nausea," I reminded her.

"Right," she said, nodding.

"Nausea?" Jay asked, grabbing the tree branch and holding it out of Kit's way.

"Thanks," she said as she scooted by. "Mom had hyperemesis when she was pregnant with me," Kit explained. "She was sick all the time and couldn't keep anything down and lost a ton of weight."

Jay nodded, his face serious. "I noticed," he said, looking at me.

It took a great deal of effort to turn away from that stare.

Rounding the last tree we were at the edge of a paved driveway alongside a small concrete block garage. I scanned our surroundings and moved cautiously toward the building, Jay and Kit quiet behind me.

A steel door sat recessed into the side of the building. I flipped up the covered panel next to the door and entered the code, hustling everyone inside. The lights came on automatically, revealing a classic jeep wrangler and little else. The walls of the garage were painted concrete and the jeep took up the majority of the interior. Along one wall there were plain white cabinets, like the kind normal people use to store tools in their garage. My tools were a little bit different.

Circling the jeep I threw open the top cabinet and began pulling down guns and clips and throwing them into my black bag. Picking up a small black handgun, I turned to Kit.

"This one is exactly like the one you use when we go to the range," I said, handing her the weapon.

Kit reached out reflexively to accept the gun then hesitated, meeting my eyes. After a moment, she said, "Ok," and took it from my hand. She checked the chamber as she'd been taught, and slipped it into her pocket.

I nodded approvingly and passed her several clips, watching as she tucked one in her opposite pocket and put the rest into her bag. From behind Kit's shoulder, I could see the conflicted expression on Jay's face and ignored him. This was not the time to debate parenting techniques.

From the lower cabinet I pulled out a set of keys and a tablet, undocking it from its charging base.

"Load up, guys," I said, turning toward the jeep.

"Shotgun," Kit called out preemptively.

I shook my head, hiding a grin as Jay climbed obediently into the back seat of the vehicle. He met my gaze in the rearview mirror and I couldn't quite interpret his expression. Giving a mental shrug I logged into the tablet as Kit fastened her seatbelt.

Opening the app for the exterior surveillance system I scrolled through the cameras and motion detection history. The men who had discovered our borrowed car had moved about halfway up the hill toward the cabin. There was no sign of any movement on this side of the property and the exterior of the garage looked completely clear.

Glancing at Kit and Jay, I turned the key in the ignition and hit the overhead button to raise the door. We all sat tensely and watched the door go up, half expecting ninjas to come flooding through the opening. As soon as the door cleared the roof of the jeep we were back on the road and rocketing toward the highway.

"Where are we going?" Kit asked.

"We need to head back to DC," Jay insisted.

I kept my eyes on the road. "You can head back to DC. I'll drop you off at the next gas station," I offered. "We're heading to Breezewood."

"What's in Breezewood?" Jay asked.

I finally met his gaze in the rearview mirror. "My Uncle Cal," I told him.

Jay's eyebrows went up. "He survived the warehouse fire?" he asked in surprise. "He was on the initial list of casualties at the time. I wasn't allowed to take part in the official investigation, of course, but I tried to get as much info as I could."

"Cal surfaced over a year later. I have no idea what went on in the meantime, but he moved his operation out to a little town in Pennsylvania. Breezewood is a major junction point between the east coast, the south, and the midwest."

Jay nodded, "All of the drugs and guns moving through this half of the country go through the 70 and 76 interchange at that little two stoplight town. There's only one reason Cal would be out there."

"Exactly." I said firmly. "I still don't know why Cal put out the original hit all those years ago. I need to find out what's going on and get him to call off this Es guy."

"If you come back with me to DC we can pull in the Organized Crime Task Force. I'm FBI now," Jay added as an afterthought.

I looked up at him in surprise. "You left the CIA? How did you find me, anyway?"

"It was dumb luck," Jay admitted. "I worked with Detective James on a case a while back and he sent me your pic after the bank robbery." Jay smirked at me in the rearview mirror. "Nice work, by the way."

"How did you end up with the FBI?" I asked, ignoring him.

Jay's smirk faded and he looked serious. I struggled to keep my eyes on the road. "After the warehouse, I needed some time. When I came back, it wasn't the same."

I glanced at him again and he caught my eyes.

"Nothing was the same," Jay said.

With effort, I pulled my gaze back to the road. I glanced over at Kit to see she was asleep again, head tilted against the window. She was still recovering from being woken up before dawn.

The silence in the car built and I let it. I was perfectly comfortable not answering the unasked question. Sadly, Jay disagreed.

"You didn't reach out to me," he said, a statement of fact that required no response on my part.

He tried again. "You could have come to me, Trixie."

I sighed, relenting. "I was going to," I told him. "Before the warehouse. I had decided to tell you everything." I carefully passed an older couple in an ancient sedan, weaving between 18 wheelers. The closer we got to Breezewood the heavier the commercial traffic became.

"After the warehouse," I began, "things were different." I glanced back to see him looking at me intently. "I had a lot of baggage." I left unsaid the extent of said baggage, including the part of it sleeping in the seat beside me.

But Jay apparently knew exactly what I meant. "It was my baggage too," he said softly.

"You had your whole life ahead of you. Your career. You didn't need to be pulled into my drama. A hit, a mob family, a truly spectacularly fucked up operation," I glanced back at him again. "And an unplanned, complicated pregnancy with an older woman."

"Older woman!" Jay scoffed. "16 months, Trixie. Get over it!" His eyes danced at me from the backseat as I felt my face get warm.

"It doesn't matter," I told him firmly. "I had to make a decision when I came out of that warehouse. I was standing in the snow, staring at the red lights and considering my options. At that moment, the best thing for me to do was disappear. So I did."

"You could have reached out to me at any time in the last thirteen years," Jay said, his voice still quiet. He sounded hurt, sad—but not angry, as I'd have expected.

"I thought about it," I told him. "A lot. Especially in the beginning. It was not a smooth pregnancy. There was a non-zero chance that Kit would make it, and I wouldn't." I met his gaze in the mirror again. "I carried your contact info with me. You were always her emergency backup."

"That means a lot to me, but you didn't have to go through that alone, Trixie. I could have been there for both of you."

"In the beginning I was just trying to make it through the pregnancy. Then I had a baby to figure out, which was not always easy," I pointed out, rolling my eyes toward Sleeping Beauty.

"Looks like you did a pretty good job there," Jay smiled, his eyes on our daughter's face.

My eyes stung and my chest felt tight. "There were days when I thought about doing a search, trying to find you. See where you were, if you were married..." I looked at him sharply. "*Are* you married?"

"Nope, not married," he answered promptly, eyes twinkling.

"Girlfriend?"

"Nope, no girlfriend either," he shook his head, a half smile lurking around his lips.

"Why not?" I asked, unable to rein in my curiosity. It belatedly occurred to me that this was not the most subtle line of questioning. My eyes flicked back up to the rearview mirror and I opened my mouth to backtrack as glass exploded around us.

Nine

Issac

"Stay on them," Issac Es said into his headset, both hands on the wheel. "I'm at mile marker 78. I'll be with you in less than 2 minutes." The sound of shots echoed over the line and he didn't expect a response. Easing on the gas as he went into another turn, Issac was aware of the men in the car behind him doing the same. This road cut like a snake through the foothills of Virginia and he was struggling to gain on Bigotti and the rest of his team as he navigated the switchbacks.

"They're returning fire," one of his agents announced as the sound of squealing tires sounded over the line, punctuated by more gunshots.

Coming out of the curve Issac laid onto the gas and raced to the next tight turn. Bagging Bigotti and her kid had become his sole focus, and the job was getting harder by the moment.

"Jacob?" Issac asked into the open line between operatives.

"Here, sir," came the immediate response.

"Try to get a pic of the male subject and send it to Kay to identify," Issac instructed.

"On it," came the expected reply.

Finally Issac rounded a tree lined curve and caught a glimpse of a black SUV up ahead. Gunning his engine, he wrung the wheel as he lost them again. Issac cursed in frustration as he had to break sharply on the switchback. Recalling the open line, he reined in his temper and reached for his usual control.

Issac's SUV roared out of the turn and he pulled up behind a matching vehicle. The front end of the other SUV was smoking and it weaved alarmingly.

"Pull off," Issac barked at Car One and the SUV immediately swerved onto the shoulder. Redlining his engine, Issac moved up behind Bigotti, who was driving an old black jeep. He could see the edge of the driver's head and a flash of movement in the backseat as a figure popped up and fired off several rounds before ducking down again.

Bigotti's new friend got a good hit at Issac's windshield, but the reinforced glass held, leaving a starburst pattern across the surface. Ignoring the damage Issac gunned the SUV's abused engine again and made contact with the back of the jeep.

He took a grim satisfaction in seeing the passengers in the jeep jolt from the impact, but it was time to end this. The sun was going down and his team had been chasing this woman since before dawn. The time for cat and mouse games was over.

"Car Two," Issac barked, "take her out."

In his peripheral vision, Issac was aware of the second SUV moving up alongside his vehicle. Glancing back quickly he noted that Car One had regained control and was now bringing up the rear.

"Car One, what's your status?" he called over the line.

"We're back in control and ready to re-engage on your order, sir," came the response.

Issac nodded in satisfaction. "Come up on the right," he instructed. "Box them in and take them out."

As they approached the next curve, Car Two slipped around Issac's vehicle to nudge at Bigotti's left flank. As the road fishtailed back in the opposite direction Car Two repeated the maneuver on the right. The road here wasn't wide enough for three vehicles abreast so Issac fell back, letting the vehicles with shooters take the lead in the chase.

The passenger in the jeep's back seat popped up again, firing off several shots, and Car One spun across the road. The front of the SUV clipped the back corner of Car Two and both vehicles were moving sideways toward the left shoulder. Issac hit his brakes hard but his momentum carried him into Car One's path. He met the horrified gaze of the driver as they made impact, then everything went black.

***

Trixie

"We're clear," Jay said from the backseat as they pulled away from the smoking vehicles.

I glanced over at Kit, who was huddled down in the passenger seat. She peeked up at me and I reached over to pat her on the leg, taking a deep breath. She slowly straightened in her seat.

"I'm awake now," she said, meeting my gaze.

I barked out a laugh, grabbing her hand and squeezing it.

"Yeah, me too," Jay agreed drily.

I let go of Kit and reached back a hand toward Jay without thinking. He grabbed it before I had time to change my mind and our eyes met in the rearview mirror.

"Thanks," I choked out, pulling my hand back.

Kit was turned in her seat, looking back at the curl of smoke still visible in the distance.

"That was a pretty good shot," she remarked.

"Thanks," Jay replied.

Sincerity rang through his voice. I caught a glimpse of his expression in the rearview mirror and had to look away. Clearing my throat, I craned my head to check the exit we were passing.

"Take this. Get off here," Jay said urgently.

I pulled off the exit, glancing back at him questioningly.

"There's a safehouse about an hour down this highway," he explained. "It's getting dark and it's been a long day. This will give us a chance to regroup and plan, okay?"

I nodded, ready for a break. I'd thought we'd get at least a good night's sleep at the cabin, so this was the next best thing.

"CIA or FBI?" I asked over my shoulder.

"Neither," Jay said, smiling mysteriously. I arched a brow at him but he just smirked back at me in the rearview mirror.

"I don't like surprises, Hot Stuff," I told him with narrowed eyes.

"I remember," he smiled widely while Kit made gagging noises from the passenger seat.

"Please, dear god, stop that," my teenager pleaded. "I've had to put up with quite a lot the last two days. There is a limit," she warned.

Not wanting to offend her delicate sensibilities any more than necessary, I continued in a more circumspect tone. "Whose safehouse is this?"

"MI6," Jay announced, taking pleasure from my obvious surprise.

"They'll give us access?" I asked. International interagency cooperation was policy in theory but not often in fact. At least not to the extent of sharing safehouses. Just the fact that Jay knew the location was unusual.

"I've got a connection," he taunted.

I rolled my eyes and let it go. I'd find out soon enough.

Jay looked away and began carefully picking the glass off the rear seat and flinging it out the window. I took stock of the jeep's condition in the wake of the firefight. We were well-ventilated but still roadworthy. I gave the dashboard a little pat and silently thanked the hardy little machine for getting the job done. Those fancy SUVs may have been bigger and newer, but it didn't look like they were coming back from that last crash. Hopefully.

"Tell me about this hired gun," I directed to Jay.

He wiped his hands on his thighs and met my gaze in the rearview mirror. "Issac Es. He's been around a while. Most of his jobs are for the South Americans but he'll work for anyone with the money."

I hated to ask this question, but... "Any connection to the Bigottis?" I didn't realize I was holding my breath until Jay shook his head.

"Not that I know of...but, Trixie, Cal has to be our top suspect. I'm sorry."

"I know," I told him. "I hate the thought that my last living relative is trying to kill me, but I'm not going to let that influence my decisions. You're right, Cal is the obvious suspect."

Kit reached over and put her hand on my arm. "He is not your last living relative. And I definitely don't want you dead."

I smiled at my kid in gratitude. Coming from a teenager, that meant a lot.

"We're family, Mom. Me and you," Kit said firmly, then cut her eyes to the man in the backseat. "And possibly him as well."

"I'm in," Jay said immediately, reaching up to put his hand on my arm above Kit's.

I caught his eyes in the rearview mirror, emotions churning, and said, "Put your seatbelt on."

"Don't worry, Jay," Kit told him, "that's definitely a sign that she cares."

I didn't know when Kit had decided to accept Jay, but I supposed, given the circumstances, that was a good thing. For the moment at least, we could use his help and resources. He'd already proven himself useful, so we might as well keep him around. Temporarily, of course.

Eyes back on the road, I rolled my shoulders and tried to relieve the stress in the back of my neck. I'd basically been driving since the early hours of the morning and I was starting to feel it.

"What exit am I looking for?" I asked.

Jay's head popped up beside me in the gap between the front seats. "It's not an exit per se," he explained. "It's basically a service road leading into the parking area for the open air amphitheater up here."

I raised my eyebrows at him.

"The venue is set in national park land," Jay explained. "Beyond the amphitheater there are several hundred acres of land, including a series of small historic houses that are used as vacation rentals. There used to be a canal system that ran all the way from DC and these cottages belonged to the caretakers. People rent them for the entire summer and write books and stuff."

"Is this the turn?" I asked, watching the signs as they went by.

"Yes, this is it," Jay directed us through the mammoth parking areas and past the empty venue. Soon we were rolling down a dirt road, tall trees arching over us on either side. Several turns later we pulled up to a small cottage situated at the edge of a brick-lined waterway. I parked the jeep as close to a large tree as I could, giving us some cover from overhead surveillance.

All three of us piled out of the jeep and converged near the passenger side rear wheel. Kit and I had our bags, Jay was empty-handed, but I knew he had at least one gun under his jacket. He'd used it to take out the men following us earlier, risking his own life.

All of my instincts were screaming at me to trust Jay, but my head kept pointing out that this was a man I didn't know. How can you trust someone with your life--with your child's life--who you haven't seen for thirteen years?

As much as I wanted to pretend I was a logical person who thought things out and made reasoned decisions, that was bullshit. I was and had always been a "fly by the seat of her pants" kind of girl. Even the decision to disappear that night thirteen years ago had been made in a moment, on pure instinct. And as much as I might try to fight against it, I was doing the same thing again. I was letting Jay into our little circle. And if he betrayed that trust they'd never find his body.

As Jay walked toward the cottage, I reached for Kit's hand and we followed behind him. Kit and I exchanged a look and I was surprised, as I always was, at how tall my baby had gotten.

Up ahead, Jay paused and I held Kit back. The door to the cottage was opening, revealing a stocky figure. I felt my mouth fly open and my lower jaw hang.

"Mitch?" I asked, stunned.

His hair was a steel gray and there were more wrinkles around his eyes, but it was definitely Mitch. For a moment we stared at each other in shock as Jay looked back and forth between us, pleased with himself.

"Hey, Kid," he said finally, smiling.

"Mitch," Jay greeted the older agent with an exuberant hand clasp. I knew Mitch had to be close to 70, but he was still a formidable figure of a man. Jay towered over him, but Mitch's shoulders were as broad and they both flexed muscled arms as they indulged in their too aggressive man-shake.

"Oh my god, Mitch, what are you doing here?" I asked, smiling at him. Mitch released Jay's hand and came out of the doorway, one arm rising to sweep me into a hug. I patted his back awkwardly and pulled back, still anchored to Kit.

"Kit, this is an old friend of mine. Mitch, this is my daughter, Katerina," I said with pride. Glancing past Mitch I caught a frown flitting across Jay's face and had a moment's guilt. I wasn't ready to introduce her as *our* daughter, at least not so casually. I didn't mean to hurt Jay's feelings, but that was a bigger conversation that would have to wait.

Kit nodded cooly to Mitch, who stood back and took her in silently for a moment.

"Wow," he said finally. "You did good, Kid." Mitch took a step closer to Kit and held out his hand. "Nice to meet you, Katerina."

Kit accepted his hand briefly, saying, "It's Kit," and took a step back.

Patting my shoulder, Mitch gestured toward the cottage's open door. "Come on in and let me show you around."

"Jay said this place is MI6...?" I let my question trail off as we all shuffled into the quaint little house.

"It is—and so am I," Mitch confirmed as he led the way into a small entryway. "On permanent loan for over three years now. It was this," Mitch waved an arm to encompass the interior of the cottage, "or they were finally going to force me into retirement."

"What, exactly, is *this*?" I asked, taking in the sparsely decorated living area. From the outside the cottage had been charming if somewhat dilapidated. The inside was similar, with the addition of a bank of high tech equipment taking up one wall. The rest of the space was a combination of living and dining rooms with an overstuffed couch at one end facing a small stone fireplace and an old white painted kitchen table at the other. One closed door sat in the wall to the right.

"This is Canal House, one of several centers set up by an interagency team focused on gathering intel on international organized crime activity. From here I monitor electronic traffic and occasionally host the odd overnight visitor. Usually witnesses being transferred from one jurisdiction to another," Mitch explained. "It's better than golf."

"Well, almost anything would be," I agreed.

Mitch led us over to the table and we all pulled up chairs.

"We thought you were dead, Trixie," he said.

I nodded, not sure where to start.

"They pulled a lot of bodies out of that warehouse," Mitch continued. "Jay and I weren't allowed to work on the investigation, but they told us about the hit that was out on you. You should have told us," he scolded.

He was right, of course, but I wasn't in the mood for the post-mortem.

"Apparently the hit is still live, because we've been running all day," I explained. "Jay said you'd put us up for the night?"

I looked at Mitch and Mitch looked at Jay, who returned Mitch's stare calmly. Finally, Mitch sighed.

"Sure," he agreed, leaning his elbows onto the table. "The bedroom is through that door. Get a good night's sleep and we'll talk in the morning."

"Thanks, Mitch," Jay said, clapping him on the shoulder.

I walked to the door with Kit at my heels. The room was barely large enough for the king size bed, a nightstand, and a small dresser. A door to the left was open and revealed a small bathroom.

"Thank god," I said, shutting the door behind us. "I've had to pee since we left the highway."

***

Jay

Watching the door close behind Trixie and Kit, Jay set aside his instinct to follow them and forced himself to turn back to Mitch.

"You knew we were coming, didn't you?" Jay asked directly, working hard to pull his attention from the bedroom door.

Mitch shrugged, "Not you, exactly, but there's been a lot of chatter in the area and I half expected it to fall into my lap." Mitch laughed and shook his head. "I never expected that girl to come back from the dead."

Sobering, Mitch pushed back from the table and crossed an ankle over his knee. "I assume that was your mess out on the highway this evening?"

"Has anyone been identified?"

Mitch shook his head. "Not yet. There was one corpse at the crash scene, no ID." He waved a hand in Jay's direction. "FBI is at the scene, so you should be able to get more info than I have."

Jay hesitated. "I haven't checked in yet." Glancing again at the closed bedroom door, Jay said, "I'm trying to get Trixie to come back to DC with me but she's determined to confront her uncle."

"I thought the uncle died in the fire?" Mitch furrowed his brow.

Jay shook his head. "Apparently he surfaced about a year later."

"Interesting," Mitch nodded. "So...what? She wants to just go up there and confront the old man face to face? With her kid in tow?"

"Our kid," Jay corrected before he could stop himself. Mitch did a literal doubletake that would have been comical under other circumstances and sat there in stunned silence.

"Well, that does change things, doesn't it," Mitch muttered as if to himself.

"It doesn't for me," Jay said. "It was always Trixie." He stopped and ran his hand over his face, pushing his hair up off his forehead. "It does change things, obviously," Jay corrected himself, "but I was always all in on Trixie. From day one ."

Ten

Issac

Issac winced as he slid his phone back into his pocket and walked across the gas station parking lot to the trio of gleaming black SUVs waiting for him. Replacement vehicles were much easier to come by than men and Issac's lips pressed tightly together.

"Call off the search," he told the woman driving the first vehicle. She nodded and lifted her hand to her earpiece as she relayed the order. Issac walked around the car and carefully maneuvered himself into the passenger seat. "Have everyone fall in," he instructed as he buckled himself in.

The SUV peeled out of the lot with the other two following closely behind. As they turned onto the highway, two more vehicles joined them and they all headed north.

***

Trixie

I looked up as Jay let himself quietly into the bedroom. The lamp beside the bed was dark but enough light spilled out of the bathroom doorway to cast a soft glow around the room. He didn't seem surprised to see me awake, but I held a finger to my lips, gesturing at Kit's inert form curled into my side.

"You need to get some sleep," he said softly, closing the door behind him and crouching beside the bed.

"So do you," I told him over our daughter's head. There were creases in the corners of his eyes that hadn't been there a couple of hours ago, but he still looked good. Damn him. Meanwhile I was fairly sure I looked like I hadn't slept for a week and I'd been living in these clothes that long too. It was a good thing I didn't care.

Jay dropped all the way down to the floor, leaning his back against the wall. "I'll take first watch. Get some sleep and I'll wake you up in a couple of hours."

I nodded. "Give me two hours and I'll be recharged," I told him, letting my head drop back down next to Kit's.

I could rarely sleep in a strange place. Usually I drifted in a half-awake trance where I could listen and monitor my surroundings but still get some rest. That's what I expected as I closed my eyes—but instead I got several solid hours of REM sleep. It was still dark when I opened my eyes but I could tell hours had passed and I felt much better.

I laid still in the bed, taking stock of the room around me. Kit was still curled against me, out for the count. I could see Jay beside the bed, his head resting back against the wall, eyes closed, lips parted. I felt my lips smile and my face soften as I watched him breathing deeply.

The crunching of tires on the dirt drive was faint, but I knew there were no other destinations anywhere near this cabin. Mitch had surveillance all over the grounds so he should be monitoring the intruder, but we still needed to be ready for company.

I frowned as I reached over to wake up Kit, once again pulling my daughter from a sound sleep to prepare for intruders. My guilt was worthless at the moment. We needed to survive this situation and—hopefully—through the other side and back to our normal lives.

Jay's head flipped down and he came awake as I touched Kit's shoulder. I shook my head at him and comprehension flitted across his face. Rising silently from the floor, he moved to the door, gun drawn from beneath his jacket.

Kit rolled toward me and our eyes met. I signaled to her to be quiet and we both moved carefully off the bed. Once we were crouched on the far side of the bed, I handed Kit her backpack and she put both straps over her shoulders. I did the same with mine and looked back at Jay, who had been watching us. He looked at me questioningly.

There were two ways we could handle this. There were windows in this room and in the bathroom that we could get out of. But Mitch was a friend and leaving out the window meant abandoning him to whoever was approaching the house from the outside.

I pulled my gun from my pocket and nodded toward the door. Jay lowered his head in acknowledgement. Turning back toward the door, Jay stood against the wall next to the door and gripped the handle, turning it slowly. Pulling the door open the smallest amount, Jay hesitated, taking in what he could see of the main room.

"Come on out, Jay." Mitch's voice cut like a knife through the silence.

Jay and I locked eyes. My brain was screaming at me in denial, but I calmly stood and walked over to join Jay at the door.

"What's going on," Kit whispered behind me.

"Mitch sold us out," I told her, not breaking Jay's gaze. I could see the torment there.

"It was my decision to come here. Stay here and let me deal with this," he told me softly.

"That's not how we do things," I told him. "I trusted Mitch too. We'll deal with this together."

"Well, I never trusted him," Kit pipped up. "He's definitely an old creeper."

I rolled my eyes at her and pressed up behind Jay at the door, a hand on his shoulder.

"We're coming out, Mitch," I called.

Jay pulled open the door several inches, taking in the scene. Mitch sat at the table where I'd last seen him, a pool of light from the fixture over the table throwing the rest of the room in shadow. Sitting in front of him on the table was a cellphone. Mitch stared at the phone, chin on his hands, elbows on the table.

Glancing back at me for a second, Jay opened the door wider and stepped through, gun still in his hand. I was right behind him, Kit's warmth at my back. We filed out one by one and approached the table where Mitch still sat, not looking up.

"Why, Mitch?" I asked him.

The door flew open and five black-clad figures entered, fanning out along each wall. Jay made a move to raise his weapon and I grabbed his arm, holding him back. With my other hand I kept Kit tucked into my side. They had us. We couldn't win a shootout right here, so we'd cooperate until we had better odds.

An armed man entered the room and walked up to the table as the phone pinged with a notification. Mitch reached forward and tapped the screen. He stared intently at the data and finally nodded. Rising from the table, Mitch pocketed the phone and picked up a bag at his feet. Pulling the bag's strap over his shoulder, Mitch finally turned his head and met my gaze. Emotions chased across his face too quickly to follow. In the end, he just looked tired.

"Sorry, Kid," he said flatly. "Don't take it personally."

"Just tell me why," I pushed, buying time .

He turned away and I called out again. "Oh, come on! Doesn't the villain need to monologue? This is your chance to defend yourself, you bastard. Let me guess, bad childhood?"

Mitch spoke without looking back. "This isn't a movie, Trixie." He glanced at the man standing at the other end of the table. "They're all yours, Mr. Es," he said, then he walked around the table and out the door.

Rage vibrated through Jay where my hand gripped his arm, but he held himself together. I felt the betrayal too, but the important thing right now was to gather as much information as possible.

The new arrival glared at me intently from the other side of the small table.

"Issac Es, I presume," I said coolly.

If Es was surprised that I knew his name, he didn't show it. He was a nondescript man in his 30s. The results of the crash out on the highway were evident across his face, but he moved smoothly.

Ignoring my gambit, Es gestured toward the door with the hand not holding a gun. "Your uncle would like to see you now,

Ms. Bigotti." The hitman stared at me with a blank, emotionless face.

"Fine," I said. "I'll go with you as soon as my companions have left the area safely." I felt Jay and Kit both tense at my words and willed them to keep quiet.

"You know that's not how this works, Ms. Bigotti," Es said dismissively.

"I know you've already lost one man out on the highway. How many more are you prepared to sacrifice?" I asked. "And for what? Cal wants me. He doesn't care about them. Let them go and I'll come with you quietly."

Es didn't react for a moment, then he raised his gun and shot. I felt Jay's entire body shudder but I didn't lose my grip on his arm. I held on as he was flung back and then began to slide down, bracing myself as his weight hit me. I struggled to keep Jay on his feet, floundering for a moment until I felt him get his feet back under himself again. I reared back, trying to see where he was hit and assess the damage.

Left bicep, flesh wound . The analytical part of my brain completed the assessment and tried to send signals to my heart and lungs to start working again. I reached for my rage to focus my emotions.

"That was a surprisingly amateurish move for an experienced professional," I pointed out to Es. "Was the corpse on the highway someone special?" I let disdain color my voice and watched in satisfaction as Es' face turned red. "Before you were just some poor SOB doing my uncle's bidding. Now it's personal ." I met his eyes. "Now I don't just want to get away from you, I want you dead."

Es was standing in the center of the room, on the other side of the table. He had five henchmen, three men and two women, spread around the room. One of the women was behind Kit, who was standing at my right shoulder. There was a man on the other side of Jay, to my left. The remaining three were arrayed behind Es on the other side of the room.

I tapped the back of Jay's arm three times, but didn't take my eyes off of Es. I tapped twice and shifted my weight to my left leg. I tapped once and released Jay, kicking out at the table as I flung my body to the right.

I didn't wait to see the table fly up into the hitman's face. Instead I was focused on raising my gun to take out the woman behind me. There was a bullet hole in her forehead and she was dropping to the ground before her gun even moved. This side of the room was clear and I pushed Kit to the floor as I swung back toward Es.

The table was on its side and there was a man and a woman advancing from behind it. I nailed the man in the chest as the woman dropped out of sight. My gaze swung to the left in time to see another man flung back against the wall with a head wound. I was vaguely aware of Jay yelling but I couldn't hear him over the ringing of the gunfire in my ears. I felt him clutch my shoulder and looked over to see him waving toward the door with his bloody arm.

Time resumed normal speed and I reached down to grab Kit's hand. She was staring at me with her mouth hanging open.

"You've got to stop doing that," she said as I pulled her to her feet.

"Doing what?" I asked, firing a shot over the top of the overturned table. A flicker of movement stopped abruptly.

"Gunfights!" she yelped, covering her ears.

"I didn't start it," I defended myself as I pushed her toward the door, right at Jay's heels. I followed her out backwards, eyes still pinned to the edges of the table. I fired a couple of shots on general principle as we burst from the cottage and into the cleared area.

I've never in my life been as happy to see a vehicle as I was that jeep, still sitting half under the tree across the clearing. I followed Jay and Kit as the three of us raced across the field, fully expecting to hear gunshots at my back at any second. Jay reached the jeep and dived through to the driver's side.

"Go, go, go!" I yelled as Kit and I crowded in behind him. In seconds he was peeling out, my ass still hanging out the door. As I clung to the door frame, I had a moment of regret that I hadn't stayed to finish the job, but it hadn't been worth the risk. I knew we'd see Es again.

Kit shimmied through the gap between the seats with some judicious pushing on my part, ending up in the back. I was finally able to pull myself completely into the seat and I slammed the door shut as we sideswiped a few trees on our way out. I turned backwards in my seat and reached back and grabbed at Kit, looking her up and down. No obvious injuries.

"You're okay?"

She nodded silently, eyes big.

I shrugged out of my backpack and passed it back to her. Next I looked at Jay, who was a little worse for wear. The side facing me seemed fine but what I could see of his left sleeve was covered in blood.

We pulled back onto the access road, which ran in a fairly straight line to the highway.

"Switch with me, Jay," I told him, grabbing the steering wheel and maneuvering myself onto his lap. He let go of the wheel and grabbed my hips. "Go," I said firmly. He gave my left hip a last pat and moved out from under me and into the other seat. I relaxed back into the driver's seat, looking over at him with narrowed eyes. Yes, the idiot was smiling at me.

"Seriously?" I shook my head at him. "Rip that sleeve off and let's see how bad this is."

"Oh my god, you were shot?" Kit cried from the backseat. She leaned into the gap between us to get a better view of Jay's arm as he began unbuttoning his shirt, revealing a white tee below it. The tee was no longer pristine, but the sleeves were short enough that it had escaped the blood from his bullet wound. Balling up the buttondown, Jay used it to clean the blood from his arm and reveal the still oozing wound.

"This isn't bad," he dismissed.

"Kit, there's a tube of skin glue in the front pocket of my bag," I told her. She fished it out and held it up to me. "I'm driving the car. You get to play Florence Nightingale."

Jay saw the look of panic on Kit's face and took mercy on her. "I can do it, Honey," he said, plucking it from her fingers.

Kit frowned at him and grabbed the small tube away from him. "I can do it."

Jay looked over at me for direction and I shrugged. "Teenager."

Accepting defeat gracefully, Jay allowed Kit to take the balled up shirt from his hands. He turned to provide her better access and sat obediently while she meticulously cleaned the wound and then glued it shut.

Hiding a smile, I said, "Mallory would be very proud of your technique."

Kit laughed, "Well, he isn't a dog, but the theory is the same."

Taking mercy on Jay, I explained, "My friend is a vet."

He nodded absentmindedly, watching Kit intently as she glued shut the wound on his bicep. "That's great," he muttered.

"That should hold," Kit told him, giving his arm the same pat she would have to a labrador.

"Thank you," Jay said sincerely.

Kit stared at him for a moment. "Thanks for your help back there," she said. "Although obviously we wouldn't have been there if you hadn't trusted that guy."

"Hey," I interrupted, "I trusted that guy, too." I pointed out. "Don't blame Jay for that. He fooled us both." I'd been trying not to think about that too much.

Jay was still turned toward the backseat. He reached across the center console with his right hand and squeezed my thigh. "Kit's right, I chose to bring us to Mitch."

I put my hand over Jay's and squeezed. His voice was flat with guilt. "I would have made the same call," I told him softly, glancing away from the road to meet his eyes. "We trusted Mitch with our lives more than once." His betrayal cut like a knife. "Honestly I'm more upset at Mitch than I am at my uncle." I shrugged at my screwy priorities and held my eyes wide to keep my emotions in check.

Kit heard the truth in my flippancy and reached through the gap in the seats to put her hand on my shoulder. Jay's hand was still on my leg and I felt overwhelmed. I took a deep breath and nodded at both of them. "Seatbelts, please."

Kit and Jay shared a glance before they both maneuvered back into their own seats and buckled up.

"You too, Mom," Kit prodded, and I reached across to strap myself in as well. We were finally back on the highway and heading north into the night.

"Are we still heading to Breezewood?" Jay asked.

"No," I told him. "Our priority has changed for the moment."

"We could head back to DC, get reinforcements," Jay suggested, but I shook my head.

"You know as well as I do that the FBI can't do anything without leverage. We're on our own."

"They could provide protection," Jay pointed out.

"I'm not interested in a new identity," I told him, glancing away from the highway for a moment to give him a meaningful look. "Been there, done that. I'm not going to run anymore."

Eleven

Trixie

I pushed open the glass door, Jay and Kit right behind me, and strode across the marble floor of the mall. Fast food restaurants lined each side of the wide hallway and the smell of french fries called to me.

"Mom?" came the voice of my clone behind me.

"No," I said firmly. We didn't have time to stop for food and we'd grabbed something on the road less than an hour ago.

Rounding the corner I spotted familiar figures standing by the large potted palm below the escalators. I raised my hand, and Mallory's eyes scanned my way. She latched onto Char and Diane and began dragging them in our direction. When Char caught sight of Kit, tears started flowing down her face and a second later the two girls were sobbing into each other's hair.

A second later I was being squeezed between Mallory and Diane, gasping for breath.

"I'm okay! I'm okay!" I reassured them, patting awkwardly at whatever part of each woman I could reach.

"Never do that again!" Mallory cried, rearing back to grab my upper arms and give me a little shake.

Diane placed her hands on Mallory's shoulders, "Don't shake her!" Diane scolded. She brushed the hair away from a bruise on my temple. "Are you okay? What happened?"

Mallory didn't give me a chance to answer. "There were police at your house!" she accused.

"I know," I told her. "We're fine," I said again. I took a deep breath and looked at each woman. "Thank you so much for coming, but I don't think this is safe for Char."

"Is it safe for Kit? Or you?" Mallory demanded.

"I brought the boys, too." Diane added. "They're around here somewhere." She gestured vaguely around her, as if expecting her four extra-large teenage sons to be crouched behind one of the potted plants.

"And I see you have brought a boy, as well," Mallory drawled, finally noticing Jay over my shoulder.

I had prepared myself for this discussion. In addition to the fact that I may be putting my best friends in danger, the major downside to asking for their help was having them ask questions about Jay that I didn't know the answers to yet.

"This is Jay—"

"My dad!" Kit interjected.

Crap. I had intended to lead into that subject gently.

Mallory and Diane were standing in front of me with their chins on the floor, their eyes flying back and forth between me and Jay. And Jay, the bastard, sidled up behind me and placed his left hand on my shoulder and extended his right out to Diane.

"Hi," he said in a rumble, "Jay Stowe, FBI. I'm honored to meet Trixie's friends."

Diane took his hand and her eyes started drifting toward half mast under the influence of Jay's deep voice. They snapped back open at his use of my real name, but Mallory beat her to the punch.

"Trixie?" she said, and they both turned their heads toward me in a coordinated exorcist-style maneuver.

I took a deep breath and fell on my sword. "I'm so, so sorry that I wasn't completely honest with you guys. Yes, my real name is Beatrix. I changed it because my Uncle Cal put out a hit on me and I was having a really rough pregnancy with Kit and I decided the safest thing for us to do was to just disappear." I ran out of steam as I ran out of air.

Mallory and Diane stared at me as several seconds ticked by.

"Say something," I demanded.

"Trixie?" Mallory repeated, then burst into laughter. She dragged me back into a hug and Diane pulled both of us into her ample bosom. I felt my throat close and rested my forehead on Mal's shoulder for a moment.

"Thank you," I whispered into her neck. I lifted my head and looked into Diane's soft brown eyes. "Thank you," I said again.

Diane leaned forward and rested her forehead against mine over Mal's shoulder. "It'll be okay," she said, "you're not alone."

I swallowed hard and cleared my throat, pulling back gently. "So yeah...Trixie." I smiled and shrugged.

"And Jay," Mallory prompted. "Any other secrets we should know about?"

"Dear god, isn't that enough?" I rolled my eyes.

"I certainly hope so!" Mallory said archly.

"She has a really cool cabin that's like built into the side of a hill," my horrible child mentioned helpfully. Kit was standing arm and arm with Char, looking at the cluster of hugging adults with a big grin on her face.

"Thank you," I said dryly. Diane turned to Kit and pulled her into a huge hug, so I felt karma had been served.

Jay leaned down and whispered in my ear, "I like your friends."

I looked back at him over my shoulder and felt a shiver pass through my body. Turning away, Mallory caught my gaze and widened her eyes eloquently. I rolled mine back at her.

"So what's the plan?" Mal asked, letting it go for the moment.

"The guy after us is a hitman who works for South American drug cartels. We need to take him out of the equation before he gets lucky."

"This is a much better plan than her original idea of single-handedly confronting the mob boss in his mountain fortress," Jay pointed out.

"Well," I admitted, "that option is still on the table." I shrugged at Jay as he narrowed his eyes at me.

"Wait! You have a hitman after you?" Mallory clutched at my arm in alarm.

"Don't worry," I told her. "He's more annoying than anything else."

"Especially since this guy has come after her three times and she's gotten away from him every time," Jay pointed out.

"You would think a professional hitman would have a higher success rate," Diane pondered.

Ignoring her, I continued. "He's been on our tail all day. I figured this was as good a place as any to confront him. We'll have the home court advantage and the crowds will hopefully inhibit his violent tendencies."

"Then what?" Mallory asked.

I smiled at the man walking toward us across the tiled floor. "Hello, Detective James. Your timing is perfect."

***

Five calls, begging, and creative threats later, I finally had a direct number to Uncle Cal. I sat in an alcove in the sun-drenched mall atrium, listening as the phone rang somewhere in Pennsylvania.

"Hello."

"Hi, Uncle Cal. It's Trixie," I answered in my most chipper voice.

There was a long hesitation on the line. I only vaguely recognized the voice as he continued, "You've caused a lot of trouble, girl."

"How?" I shot back, "And to whom?"

"To me, you little bitch," he bit out. "Why aren't you dead yet?"

"Wow. That took a turn. What did I ever do to you?" I asked sincerely.

"You didn't die. I just need you dead, you stupid girl," he snarled.

"So sorry to disappoint, Uncle Cal." Had I really been looking for some kind of explanation that made sense? After all these years, it didn't even matter. He wanted me dead. I refused to accommodate him. It was a classic impasse. "How's your boy Issac doing? He's getting pretty beat up in this game. You may need to send him back to the minors."

"Don't worry about Mr. Es. He'll get the job done. He knows the consequences for failure," the voice rumbled, then the line clicked and went dead.

"I'm sorry," Jay said, seated next to me on the bench.

I shook my head, waving my hand dismissively. "It doesn't matter. It's not like we were close, anyway. It's just weird not knowing why." I pushed those feelings aside and cleared my throat. "But I'm sure Mr. Es is now headed in this direction, which was the real point of that call, family drama aside." I smiled as I rose from the bench and turned back to offer Jay my hand.

"Shall we?" I asked, as he stood up beside me.

"Absolutely," Jay responded, squeezing my hand.

We returned to the cafe area in the center of the mall where Mal, Diane, Char, and Kit waited for us at two small tables. Jay and I sat at the next bench, beside Kit and Char. Mal immediately began moving her table toward the girls'.

"Bring it in," she commanded. I rolled my eyes at Jay but scooted our table toward Kit's until all three were pressed together. Mal leaned over the newly constructed uber-table and scream-whispered, "How did it go?"

"Mission accomplished," I confirmed. "Now we just have to see how long it will take him to get here. I don't think he was far behind us."

Char tapped Mallory on the shoulder, "You're practically in my lap, mom!"

Mallory ignored her but leaned back a little.

"The boys are all in place," Diane interjected soothingly. It turned out she hadn't just brought her four huge teenage sons—she'd brought their entire football team in her sprinter. We had an army of testosterone at our disposal. "They have eyes on every entrance and they'll ping us if they see someone who looks out of place."

I nodded gratefully. Jay was right, this was a much better plan than trying to face Cal alone.

Suddenly everyone's phones pinged in unison. Mallory had hers in her hand. "Dean sent a picture," she announced. I pulled my phone from my pocket and opened the app to see a picture of a man dressed in black tactical gear walking through one of the department store entrances. Another ping popped up a similar picture at the main mall entrance. I'd barely opened that image when a photo of yet another figure all in black popped up, this time at the entrance near the movie theaters.

"They're here," I said calmly, standing. "Does everyone know their part?"

The faces that looked up at me were nervous, some pale, but they seemed confident—both in themselves and in me.

"I love you guys," I said sappily, before I could stop myself. I saw several smartass comments bubbling to the surface and cut them off at the knees. "No," I said firmly, holding up a finger. "Everyone go." To my amazement, they all rose without a word and scattered toward their assigned positions.

I started toward the far end of the mall, Kit falling in at my side.

"I like him," Kit burst out.

I didn't have to ask who she meant.

"Really?" I asked. "You're a teenager. You're not supposed to like anyone."

Kit rolled her eyes at me. "Well, I hate to damage my reputation, so don't tell anyone." She looked over at me, trying to catch my eye. "But I do," she said sincerely. "I like him and I like how he treats you. I will absolutely deny this, but you guys are kind of cute together."

I looked at her aghast. "Cute?"

"Trixie and Jay, sitting in a tree..." the horrible child began singing at me.

"Cut it out!" I scolded her. "Time to get serious. Bad guys are in the building."

Kit had the sense to at least give me a sheepish look. "Yes, ma'am."

I shook my head at her nonsense as we approached the ticket desk for the movie theater. I used my credit card to buy two seats and we got in line to enter the lobby area.

A tinny voice sounded from above. *Issac Es, please meet your party in theatre 8.* The announcement repeated once more as we moved through the line and into the theatre.

I joined the line at the lobby counter, keeping an eye out on the main entrance and the hallway leading back to the actual theaters. When it was our turn I bought a bottle of water and a large popcorn, which I handed to my grateful child.

"Oh my god, I love you."

"You're welcome," I told her, my eyes on a figure entering the lobby. "And there's our man. Let's go."

Stuffing napkins into my pocket, I pulled Kit away from the counter and down toward the theaters. We slipped into number eight and paused in the darkness to let our eyes adjust. The movie was already playing and the theater was pitch black except for the light from the screen. I grabbed a handful of Kit's popcorn and scattered it in front of the door. Pushing her down the first aisle, I continued to spread popcorn until we reached the end of the row.

We quickly slipped down the gap between the end of the rows and the wall, abandoning the tub of popcorn and wiping our hands on the napkins. Footsteps crunched behind us as we rounded the corner to the emergency exit alcove. I glanced back as I pushed Kit through the door and a silhouetted figure moved down the center aisle at a run.

I slipped through the door after Kit and a hand pulled me to the side. The body I fell into felt surprisingly familiar. I looked up in the dim light of the access hallway into Jay's face. He was staring down at me intently.

"He's right behind us," I whispered urgently as Jay pulled me further from the door. I looked over his shoulder to see Kit standing behind him. All three of us moved to the right to watch the show.

Issac pushed through the door and stumbled to a halt, taking in the wall of uniformed police officers arrayed across the hallway. Detective James stepped forward, his weapon in his hand.

"On the ground, hands behind your head," he said firmly.

For a moment, Issac didn't move. His face was frozen and revealed nothing of the wheels that must have been turning. Finally, it was as if the air had been let out of his tires. Issac seemed to sag. The tension drained from his body and he slipped gracefully to his knees, lowering his body to the floor.

Detective James holstered his weapon and grabbed Issac's wrists to place him in cuffs. He pulled a handgun from a shoulder holster under Issac's jacket, a knife from his waist, and another gun from his ankle.

"Anything else you want to tell me about now?" he asked Issac, leaning down over his prone form.

"No," Issac said shortly. James nodded and two uniformed officers stepped up to haul Issac to his feet and lead him down the tunnel. James' partner followed behind, reading his Miranda Rights.

Twelve

Trixie

I looked up at Jay. "Well, that was disturbingly easy."

Kit piped up, "Disappointingly anticlimactic, really."

I nodded in agreement at her while Jay rolled his eyes and shared a look of commiseration with Detective James.

"Are we free to go, Detective?" I asked.

James gave me some impressive side-eye and ignored me to ask Jay, "Besides the two stolen cars and the unidentified bodies in the government facility—which are not my problem, thank god—is there anything else you or Ms. Welsh need to tell me?"

"Nope," Jay said immediately, "that's it."

James looked over at me consideringly, then nodded to Jay. "I'll keep you looped in on what we learn from our new friend,

Mr. Es." With that the Detective turned away and strode quickly after the other officers.

Jay, Kit, and I walked back down to the central cafe below the skylights to find a gaggle of teenagers demolishing a cardboard box of fancy cookies with Mallory and Diane playing referee.

"I saved you the last pink one," Char cried, upon seeing Kit. The two girls oohed and ahhed over the fancy decorated cookie as Jay and I flung ourselves into two seats across from each other.

"They got him?" Mallory asked, leaning toward our table. I nodded, reaching for a cookie. Diane slid the box closer and I grabbed two, passing one to Jay.

"The cops picked up all of the guys we were following, too. They all just gave in." She shrugged, obviously disappointed not to have seen a bloody battle to the death. "So what's next?"

"We wait to hear from Detective James. It may take him a couple of days to get Issac to talk," Jay cautioned.

"I doubt it. Issac looked ready to call it a day," I pointed out as Jay's phone vibrated where he had sat it on the table.

"It's James," he said, picking it up. "Everything okay, Detective?"

Jay listened for a moment and answered, "Of course, I understand. We'll both be there." He ended the call and met my curious gaze. "The detective wants us in his office first thing tomorrow."

I nodded as Diane's phone buzzed on the neighboring table. She glanced down at the screen and smiled.

"Doug is firing up the BBQ," she announced. "Let's roll, team!" A horde of extra large teenage boys raised their arms and cheered and rallied around Diane as she rose from her seat across from Mallory. Like a suburban Brunehilde, Diane prepared to lead her troops from the mall, stopping at our table to press my hand. "You're coming, right?" she asked. Glancing at Jay, she added firmly, "All three of you."

I sighed and looked over at Jay, tilting my head inquiringly and half shrugging a shoulder.

Jay leaned forward and smiled. "I'd love to," he said firmly.

I nodded at Diane. "We'll be there. We'll stop and grab dess ert...ice cream?"

"Oh, you don't hav—"

"Yes, please!" her oldest interjected, leaning over her shoulder to cut his mom off. She reached up to ruffle his hair and rolled her eyes, smiling.

"Sure. Thank you! But don't take a lot of time, okay? We'll be waiting for you." I nodded as Diane pulled me into a quick hug and led her troops off toward the parking garage.

I looked over at Mallory to see her watching me with narrowed eyes. "What?" I said, innocently.

"Nothing," she answered, smiling and turning to Kit. "Hey, Kit, why don't you ride with me and Char?" Mallory grabbed her bag and got to her feet, Char following her. "That way we can be sure your mother won't disappear on us again," she finished.

I stuck my tongue out at her and flipped her off.

"No, but I promise we'll be there," I told her. "You'll just have to trust me."

Mallory leaned in for a hug, whispering in my ear, "I like him," before hustling her daughter away.

And just like that it was the three of us again. Two parents with their teenager, at the mall. *My brain hurts*. This was all a bit much and a bit too fast for me. I couldn't imagine what it felt like for Jay.

"You don't actually have to come to Diane's if you don't want to. They're absolutely planning a thorough interrogation. Remember that guy who wanted to cut off your eyelids in Istanbul? I'm pretty sure he's Mallory's third cousin on her mother's side."

Jay smiled at me. "Sounds fun. I wouldn't miss it for the world."

"Your funeral," I said flippantly but inside I was definitely panicking. Turning to Kit, who was watching the exchange as if it were a tennis match, I put a hand over hers on the table. "Ready to head out, Kitten?" She nodded and we all rose silently and headed to the garage.

As I pulled the jeep onto the highway to head back to our neighborhood, I glanced at Kit in the rearview mirror. "You're awfully quiet back there. Everything okay?"

"I don't know," Kit answered honestly. "Is it over? Everyone's acting like it's over but it doesn't feel like it. What about Uncle Cal? Won't he just hire another guy like Issac?"

Jay turned in his seat, resting his elbow on the center console so he could address Kit directly. "No, you're right," he told her, "it isn't over. But it's out in the open now and we should get a bit of a break before we have to deal with Cal's next move. And we're going to try everything we can to block it before it happens."

Kit nodded in understanding, a little of her tension draining away.

"Luckily, there aren't a lot of guys like Issac," Jay continued. "The others who might be thinking about taking Cal's money will know pretty quickly what happened. Cal should have a pretty hard time finding someone else to do his dirty work."

"That's good," she said, sounding more herself.

We exited the highway and made the first turn into the small shopping center that housed our neighborhood grocery store. Piling out of the vehicle again, the three of us continued our nuclear family cosplay into the store in search of ice cream. As Kit ran ahead down the aisle, Jay walked at my shoulder. I could sense him looking down at me and I worked hard at ignoring him.

"James asked me to stay with you tonight," he said abruptly, and I finally looked at him, eyebrows raised. "He said he could arrest you but he was going to trust me to make sure you didn't disappear again."

"Well, he and Mallory are on the same page then, aren't they." I rolled my eyes. "Geez. You disappear and assume a fake identity *one time...*"

"I'll sleep on the couch, you'll never know I'm there," he said earnestly.

"It's okay, Jay. I'm not mad."

We'd reached the ice cream aisle and I turned toward him at the corner and walked backward down the aisle a few steps. "I don't actually hate having you around." I flipped around and jogged a few steps to catch up to Kit, whose head was buried in a freezer. She popped out with three cartons she promptly dumped into my arms and went back in for more.

Within minutes we were back in the car and heading deeper into the neighborhood. After a brief discussion we decided to leave the jeep in my driveway and walk across the park to Diane's. Walking up the driveway, arms laden with cartons of ice cream, the three of us could hear the sounds of what had definitely evolved into an actual party coming from the back of the house. We let ourselves into the gate to the backyard and were immediately mobbed by Mallory's Danes.

"Well, hi!" Jay laughed, keeping his feet in a display of impressive fortitude. "Who do we have here?"

"This is Rosie," I cuddled the big block head that swung my way at the mention of her name, "and that's Roscoe. They're Mal's."

"They're gorgeous," Jay said as Mallory and Char walked up.

"Thank you," Mal said without modesty. She plucked the ice cream out of my arms and handed it off to Char, then pulled me into a tight hug for a moment. Then she reared back and held me by my upper arms while looking into my eyes intently. "I am so glad you're okay."

Diane popped up behind her shoulder and pulled me away and into her ample bosom. "Me too!" she cried.

"Me too!" called a voice from the other side of the yard.

I looked up to see Diane's husband, Doug, waving a BBQ implement wildly in my direction. I laughed and waved back.

"Thanks, Doug!"

"Doug wants to meet Jay," Diane said, grabbing Jay by the arm and pulling him away abruptly. I caught his slightly wide-eyed glance back in my direction and adjusted my wave in his direction, smiling widely.

Kit and Char had disappeared somewhere with the ice cream, which left me at Mallory's mercy.

"We're going to sit down and you're going to explain to me exactly what has been going on for the last two days," Mal said firmly, guiding me to the patio table.

I glanced around, checking in on Jay, who was standing by the grill with Doug and another couple, and Kit, who was standing in a circle of teenagers nearby. My other neighbors, a really nice older couple with two grown children who'd moved away, were seated by the pool chatting and waved when they caught my eye. It looked like any of Diane's normal Friday night neighborhood parties and the abrupt switch from being shot at to suburban socialization was giving me a bit of a headache.

"I'm not sure there's much to tell," I said to Mal. "I told you I was with the CIA—"

"No, you just said the government. You were a secret agent?" Mal accused.

"I was an *agent*," I corrected, rolling my eyes, "But it doesn't matter. None of this really has anything to do with the CIA." I sagged back into my chair, letting some of what I was feeling color my voice. "My uncle put a hit out on me," I said abruptly. "When the police figured out who I was after the robbery, it raised a flag. Apparently he's still got it in for me after thirteen years," I said, grimacing.

Mallory was looking at me with wide eyes. "Your uncle..." she said slowly, "put out a *hit* on you?" She paused as if parsing each word. "Like a mob hit? Like your father's brother hired a hitman to kill you?"

I sighed, resting my elbows on the table and pressing my fingertips to my eyes. A second later I felt Mallory's arm around my shoulders and I took a deep breath.

"I'm okay," I told her, raising my head. "But yeah, that's pretty much the gist of it."

"I'm so sorry, Annie," Mal said softly, rubbing her hand across my back. She froze. Her eyes narrowed but I could see the smile lurking around her mouth. "That's right, I'm still mad at you! You left out a pretty big detail...Trixie!"

I rolled my eyes. "You can still call me Annie—it's fine!" I shook my head. "No one's called me Trixie for thirteen years before today. It feels weird." I hesitated, poking at my feelings like a sore tooth. "Good, but weird."

"I like Trixie," Mallory said firmly. "But I'll probably slip and call you Annie still. You know how I feel about change."

"Oh, yes," I assured her. "We're all well aware."

"Now that we have that settled, what exactly happened the other night? We woke up to cops all over the neighborhood and poor Mr. Blume's car was stolen."

Oh, crap.

"Umm..." I hesitated, my face getting warm. "That was me. But the car is fine and I'm sure the police are bringing it back to him."

"Oh. My. God." Mallory breathed, looking around to make sure no one else was listening. "Seriously? You stole Mr. Blume's car? His precious electric car that he's mentioned at least twice in the neighborhood newsletter. Oh, man. You are definitely going to hell."

I shrugged. "Armed men broke into the house to kill us. It was take the car or stage a shootout and you know I just finished redoing the kitchen."

Mallory nodded sagely, understanding the time, money, and emotional investment I'd put into the new kitchen.

"So instead of trying to make a stand at the O-K Corral," I continued, "we staged a quick retreat. I took Kit to a place I have out in the country. Jay found us there."

"Yes," Mal drawled, "Let's talk about Jay."

Diane slid into the chair beside me. "Ooh, I got here just in time for the good stuff," she said gleefully, giving a little bounce in her seat.

I fought the urge to drop my head to the table. I guess I owed them this.

"So, yes," I started, "Jay is Kit's father and yes, we had a relationship many years ago." I sighed, looking down at the tabletop.

"He was CIA too?" Mal asked.

I nodded.

"But when I realized the hitman had nothing to do with my work, I didn't want to involve him."

"Hitman?" Diane interrupted.

"Her uncle hired a hitman. Keep up, Diane," Mal started to wave a hand dismissively and froze and turned back to me with a frown. "But you never said why."

"I don't know why," I admitted quietly. "When I tried to ask him he wasn't really interested in chatting." The memory of dancing flames and screams ran through my head.

"When I realized how much danger we were in, I made the decision to leave. I had an opportunity and I took it."

"You didn't talk to Jay first?" Diane said without rancor.

"No. We hadn't made any kind of commitment--I hadn't actually seen him for months. And he is younger than I am. And let's face it, ridiculously hot. He hasn't changed a bit, damn it." The three of us turned to take in the sight of Jay, still standing at the grill with Diane's husband, who was rather round. Doug was an awesome guy, and gave great hugs, but no one was ever going to describe him as *hot*. One of our other neighbors had joined their conversation, sporting the typical dad bod with a third trimester belly and a stark sock tanline.

Jay was still wearing his slightly dingy white t-shirt. The white of the bandage around his bicep blended into the sleeve and wasn't obvious. The cut of his trousers was a much bigger distraction as they pulled taut over his glutes. Jay shifted position, causing his muscles to flex and all three of us sighed.

"So not only was I older and knocked up, but I had a ton of baggage. It was easier to just disappear and deal with my problems on my own," I concluded.

"Well, it's good to know you haven't changed at all in thirteen years," Mallory rolled her eyes at me.

I shrugged off the implied criticism.

"I had to make a quick decision. I'd gone to see my uncle and the whole fucking building exploded. It was snowing and the building was on fire and it was the perfect opportunity for me to disappear. I took it." I could still remember how cold I'd felt, my feet already turning numb as I stood in the snow and stared at the flashing lights in the distance. "You guys have never seen me really sick. Pregnancy—and not being able to keep anything down—knocked me on my ass." And I wasn't about to second guess my decisions at this point. The only thing I had to do now was decide where I was going from here.

"I'm sorry, Annie," Mallory squeezed my hand. "I can't imagine how hard that was."

"And you did a great job building a life for you and Kit," Diane added.

"Damn straight, I did," I said as a huge yawn caught me off guard. I scrubbed my face, the last two days catch up with me. I regretted not driving the car over.

A familiar weight draped itself across my back and Kit's head hung down over my shoulder. "Carry me home, Mom."

"Oh, hell, no," I laughed. I dropped a loud kiss onto her head and shoved her off so I could stand up. Kit flipped her hair back and stood up. She laughed but I could see the exhaustion in her face too. I looked around for Jay. A hand touched my waist and just like that, he was there.

"Hi," I said softly.

"Hi, yourself," he answered. "Ready to head home?"

"Absolutely."

The walk through the park was mostly a blur. I was so tired it was an effort to keep my eyes open at this point, although Kit seemed to perk up, maintaining a running commentary the whole time. Finally we turned onto the brick paved walk leading to our front door and I dug out my key.

"Someone cleaned," Jay said, as I switched on the light.

"Diane," I told him as Kit sprinted up the stairs to check her room. "She mentioned it when I called her this morning. She has a key. She checks on the house when we're away and sometimes she just needs to come and hide from the testosterone in her house."

"All of those boys aren't hers, though, right?"

"Not by birth, but they're pretty much always at her house. Doug coaches the team."

"He mentioned that. They seem really nice. I like your friends." Jay smiled down at me.

"Yeah, me too. We've been really lucky," I smiled back. Nodding down at the couch, I said, "Let me grab you some blankets. I'll be right back." I walked up the stairs, the weight of Jay's gaze following my every step.

Poking my head in Kit's room, I found her sitting on the bed and rifling through the top drawer of her nightstand.

"Everything okay?"

"Yeah," she sighed. "Everything is moved, but I don't think anything is missing."

"That's good. Can you grab an extra pillow from the top shelf of your closet and take it down to Jay, please?"

"Sure, Mom."

"Thanks, Kitten." I continued down the hall to the linen closet. A moment later I was back downstairs with a stack of relatively fresh linens and presented them to Jay.

"Here's a blanket and a sheet. Kit will bring you down a pillow."

"This is great, thank you," Jay said, accepting my offering.

I gestured toward the leather sofa, "It's actually really comfortable. I fall asleep on it all the time."

"She snores," came a voice from the staircase.

"I don't," I said calmly to Jay.

"You do when you fall asleep on the couch," pointed out the horrible beast, approaching with a pillow.

"Only on the couch," I assured him as he laughed at both of us.

"It's okay," Jay said.

"Thank you," I replied, turning away and walking up the stairs without looking back at either of them. I was way too tired for this. It had been an amazingly exhausting three days with basically no sleep. I trudged into my room, toed off my shoes, and fell into bed. I'm pretty sure I was asleep before I hit the mattress. And I didn't snore.

Thirteen

Jay

Jay reached for his phone, surprised to see Detective James was calling so early. Propping himself up on the arm of the couch, he spoke quietly, aware Trixie and Kit were still asleep above him. "Good morning, Detective."

"That's a subject for debate. I've been up with our friend all night," James responded.

"And did your night owl sing?"

"Chorus and verse," James replied with satisfaction. "And what a song it is. I assume you knew about Calvin Bigotti's involvement?"

"I had reason to suspect that might be the case, but no proof," Jay swerved.

James harrumphed. "And of course you knew that our Ms. Welsh is Mr. Bigotti's niece."

"I think you know more about Cal Bigotti than I do. All I know is what Trixie had suspected twenty years ago."

There was a moment of silence and then James sighed, "Well, give me a couple of hours to recharge and I'll fill you in. We've got enough to take this guy down for good. My office, 10 o'clock?"

"We'll be there," Jay confirmed before making his goodbyes and ending the call. He caught a flash of movement from the corner of his eye and looked up to see Trixie standing on the staircase. "Good morning," he said quietly, smiling.

***

Trixie

I returned Jay's smile, continuing down the stairs.

"We're meeting the detective at 10am," he said.

"You should call me Anne," I said abruptly. Jay looked surprised, but after a moment's hesitation he nodded.

"Ok," he agreed, "If that's what you want." Jay stood from the couch and came to meet me at the foot of the stairs. We were both speaking softly, as if we might wake up a teenager at dawn.

"It may take me a while to get used to Anne. I've been thinking of you as Trixie for a long time."

"Have you?" I said softly, "Been thinking about me, I mean."

"I have," he whispered back, stepping in closer. I pressed a hand firmly against his chest, halting his forward motion.

"I think you have something of mine," I said, raising one brow. Jay looked at me blankly until I raised my other hand, showing him the empty picture frame from my bedroom. Comprehension gave way to an endearingly sheepish smile.

"Guilty," he conceded. Jay's expression became intent and he met my eyes. "Can I keep it? At least long enough to make a copy?"

I could tell this meant a lot to him and I felt my throat start to close. I couldn't push out the words, so I nodded.

"Thank you," Jay said sincerely, putting his hand over mine where it still rested against his chest.

He leaned in to press a kiss to my lips and the quiet noises of the morning disappeared as the world around us ground to a halt. I felt his breath catch against my lips as he paused, pulling back until our lips barely touched, and my entire body moved forward, desperate not to lose that connection.

Jay met me halfway, and our hands were caught between our bodies. He felt so warm and solid against me and I couldn't help giving into that feeling for a long moment. But my daughter was asleep upstairs and as much as I'd been trying to forget it, I still had to deal with the mess I'd left behind thirteen years ago. As good as this felt, it wasn't the time...*yet?*

I pulled back, fighting my own instincts as I pushed back against Jay's chest to create some space between us. It felt like I had to pry my eyes back open, but finally I looked at Jay's face—only to see his eyes locked onto my lips.

"Breakfast," I blurted. I sidestepped around him and headed to the kitchen. After a long moment, Jay sighed and followed me.

"Eggs? Toast?" I called over my shoulder, firmly moving on.

"Anything you decide is fine," Jay said meaningfully, grabbing a stool on the other side of the island.

I took a deep breath and stood on the other side of the island, hands braced on the cool marble top. I met Jay's gaze with effort. "What's your plan, Hot Stuff?"

"For today?" he asked. "We're going to meet with the detective and come up with a plan to deal with your uncle. Permanently."

"And after that?"

Jay smiled. "You're the one who always has plans within plans. You tell me."

I glared at him in frustration.

"I meant what I said," Jay continued. "Whatever you decide is fine with me. I'm going to follow your lead."

"And if I lead you right over a cliff?"

"Then I'll hold on tight as we go down," he said.

I threw my hands up and turned away from him to bury my head in the refrigerator.

"That is so not helpful," I muttered under my breath as I pulled out bacon and eggs.

Ten minutes later the smell of bacon had made its way upstairs and rousted the teenager out of bed. She presented herself for breakfast in a badly rumpled tee and pj pants covered in pineapples, her hair flat on one side.

"Have you brushed your teeth?" I asked on autopilot. Kit gave me a blank look. I shrugged and sat a plate of food in front of her at the island, beside Jay. I was leaning on the other side, shoveling eggs into my mouth as if I hadn't eaten in weeks. Jay had finished off an alarming amount of bacon, necessitating a second batch.

"Do you have parents?" Kit asked abruptly. "Living, I mean." It took my brain a second to process that she was asking Jay.

He popped the last piece of bacon into his mouth and wiped his face with a napkin before responding.

"I do," he said. "My parents live in North Carolina. Would you be interested in meeting them?" He asked carefully.

"Would they be interested in meeting me?" Kit threw back at him.

"Definitely, yes," Jay responded without hesitation. "My parents would absolutely love to meet you. One of the greatest disappointments of their lives is that I haven't provided them with grandchildren. My mom is the president of the ASPCA down there and I don't even have a dog. I'm a total failure in their eyes. You could be my redemption."

"Geez, no pressure or anything," Kit rolled her eyes. "I'll think about it," she told him firmly.

"Do I get any input into this decision?" I asked archly. They both turned to look at me, staring at me with the same eyes, and suddenly I needed to be elsewhere. I dropped my plate into the sink and scurried from the kitchen like a rat deserting a sinking ship.

Kit caught me halfway up the stairs, practically tackling me into a hug. I turned in her arms to wrap around her, pulling her into my stomach. I was a step above her, which put her at the perfect height for a good mom hug.

"I'm sorry," she said into my stomach. "I didn't mean to upset you. We totally don't have to meet them."

"It's okay," I told her, rubbing her shoulders. "If you want to meet them, we can."

Kit looked up at me, tears in her eyes.

"It's okay, baby," I said again, holding her tight. We stood there for a long moment. When I opened my eyes, Jay was standing at the foot of the stairs, looking up at us with pain in his eyes. "It's okay," I said, looking at him.

"It's like I've been on autopilot for the last thirteen years," he began slowly. "It's like part of me knew I was just waiting for you to come back."

He looked down for a moment and when he met my gaze again, his eyes were fierce. "I'm so sorry, Trixie--Annie--I'm so sorry that I didn't try to find you. Because in my heart, I think

I knew all along that you were out there. And I just waited for you to find me."

"You waited?" I asked.

Jay took a step up the staircase. "I didn't date. I wasn't kidding about being a disappointment to my parents. My dad gave me this whole speech about them still loving me if I was gay and how they'd welcome a son-in-law. They really are completely desperate for me to settle down." Jay took a deep breath and another step. "But it was always you. Whether you want me to call you Trixie or Annie, or Bob. It was always you."

Jay took another step closer and Kit thrashed in my arms. "Oh my god, let me out, let me out! Don't you guys dare kiss in front of me!"

The horrible child wiggled away, making dramatic gagging noises and dashed up the stairs, abandoning me in my moment of need. I threw my hands up, looking at Jay—and we burst into laughter.

Jay bounded up the last couple of steps between us and swept me into his arms. I ran my hands across his shoulders, still standing a step above him so that we were eye to eye. His body was solid and warm under his shirt and I explored the muscles there.

"We're right back where we started this morning," I said softly.

"Good," Jay said firmly. "This is my new favorite place." His smiling lips met mine again and everything fell away. I knew there were a lot of things unsettled, not the least of which was what to do about Cal, but for the moment I leaned into the warmth of this man. Thirteen years is a long time to pretend not to miss someone.

A buzz from Jay's watch pulled us apart.

"It's 9:30. We need to meet Detective James at 10 or he's going to send a SWAT team after us," Jay said apologetically.

"We'll be ready to go in ten minutes," I said, turning to head back up the stairs.

True to my word, I was heading back down the stairs nine minutes later. Jay's car had been delivered sometime in the night and he'd changed his shirt from the emergency clothes in the trunk, but hadn't bothered with a jacket. His shirtsleeves were rolled up and several buttons were undone at his neck. I made a determined effort to ignore the column of warm skin exposed at his neck.

Kit and I had both changed into jeans. She'd paired hers with a tee decorated with a drawing of a dog as a potato and I was wearing a simple black cross wrap top with a tie at the waist. Jay waited for us at the bottom of the stairs, shrugging into his jacket, and it seemed so natural to flow into his arms for a quick hug.

Catching the side-eye from my child, I pulled back and grabbed my bag from the side table as I swung open the door. My eyes met Jay's as the light from the open door swept across his face. His eyes closed and his body moved backward, head falling forward. The sound of the gunshot caught up to me a moment later as my brain struggled to process what I was seeing.

"Run!" I shouted to Kit, who was still standing on the bottom step. She turned and scrambled back up the stairs, hands clawing for purchase.

Jay, on the floor behind me, and Kit, cresting the top of the staircase, were burning embers in my mind as I forced myself to turn to the open door and assess the threat. I had to buy Kit time. The back of my brain was clawing at me to go to Jay but even after all of this time my training wouldn't let me turn my back on the threat outside of the door.

The morning light bathed the lush suburban neighborhood in green and gold. The men in black combat gear and automatic weapons standing on my front lawn had no place here. My hands twitched but I had no weapon on me or anywhere near. I hadn't seen Jay's gun but it was most likely on him. I froze as a familiar figure stepped out from behind the big oak tree next to my driveway.

"Your uncle would like to see you, Trixie," Butch said calmly. A black SUV pulled up to the curb behind him and Butch stood there, as if he had all of the time in the world. He hadn't aged a day in the years since I'd seen him.

The two men in combat gear stepped closer and my window of opportunity closed. All of my senses were focused on the silence echoing through the house.

Making a decision, I stepped forward slowly, onto the slatted wood planks of my front porch, and pulled the door of the house closed behind me. I felt the click of the lock like a jolt through my entire body but kept my eyes steady on Butch. One foot in front of the other I moved across the porch and down the three stairs to the sidewalk. Every step away from the house holding Jay and Kit felt like I was wading through mud, but I pushed on, pulling the focus away from them.

Step by step I walked past the men with the automatic weapons and down my driveway. Butch opened the car door for me and I slid inside. A moment later he slid into the front seat beside the driver and the car shot forward from the curb. As we rounded the corner I caught a glimpse of the two other men piling into a matching SUV. They pulled onto the road behind us and my heart started beating again. At least Kit was safe.

***

Kit

From her vantage point under her mother's bed, Kit held her breath and let it out slowly. With every exhale dust bunnies floated around her face, but she didn't move. Her heart was pounding so loudly in her ears that she would miss an elephant stampeding up the stairs at this rate. Focusing on slowing down her breathing, she stared at the tiny slice of the hallway she could see from her hiding spot.

Seconds passed like hours, but there were no sounds beyond the normal neighborhood noises. Cars passed, dogs barked.

Everything within the house was still. Slowly, her body began to relax. She let her head fall forward and rested her forehead on the dusty floor as her mind raced. She'd seen Jay fall and assumed he'd been shot. She didn't know if he was downstairs still, and possibly hurt, and she didn't know where her mother was. At this point, if her mother hadn't followed her up the stairs, Kit had to assume she'd been either hurt or taken.

Eyes closed, Kit considered her options. Staying here wasn't one of them. She could try to escape through the back gate, the same way she and her mother had left the house last time. But after that she didn't know where she'd go. Maybe circle back to Char's house? But as far as Kit was aware, Char's mom didn't even own a gun and that might be putting them in danger. Second option, go downstairs and call the police. Kit had left her phone on the table beside the door. Assuming it was still there.

Jay might also still be downstairs. He might be hurt. He might be dead. Either way, Kit needed to know.

Decision made, Kit worked her way to the door of the room and peered around the frame to the top of the steps. On her hands and knees, Kit moved into the hallway. At the top of the stairs she gazed down to see the front door closed and the room looking completely normal--except for the men's shoes visible at the left edge of her view.

Kit froze for a moment, then launched herself down the stairs. Jay's body came into view as she descended the stairs. He wasn't moving, but there was no blood or sign of a wound.

Kit hovered over him, hands above his chest, then took a deep breath and dropped her hands onto him and shook.

"Jay?" Kit's voice broke and she cleared her throat and tried again more firmly. "Jay!"

Looking at where her hands rested on the front of his jacket, Kit felt something hard and noticed the small, dark hole burned into the fabric. Flipping the jacket open she dug into the pocket and pulled out the remains of a cell phone. One of the pieces clearly had a round divot notched out along the broken edge. "Jay!" Kit said again, accompanied by a firm shake. "Dad!"

Jay's back arched off of the floor and he gasped for air. Kit felt lightheaded with relief and allowed herself to fall back onto her butt, hands on her forehead.

"Oh, thank god," she said to herself, holding back tears.

Taking a deep breath, Kit jumped to her feet and ran into the kitchen to grab a bottle of water. She detoured to grab her phone on the way back and collapsed again at Jay's side. He was pushing himself up and Kit put an arm around him, maneuvering herself under his shoulder to help him up.

Once Jay seemed reliably upright, Kit sat back and opened the bottle of water, handing it to him silently. Jay took a long drag of water as his eyes darted around the room.

"They took her?" he finally asked.

Kit shrugged, fighting back tears again. She swallowed hard before answering. "I think so."

When Jay patted his pocket, Kit gestured to the pieces of his phone on the floor beside them and handed him hers. Jay accepted the offered phone and placed it on his lap to reach out and pick up one of the broken pieces. Turning it over in his hands he traced the round divot with a finger. Jay looked up at Kit, who nodded. The tears in her eyes spilled over when Jay wrapped his arm around her, pulling her into his chest.

Kit let herself cry, leaking her fear and worry onto Jay's previously pristine white shirt before pulling herself together and sitting back. Gesturing to the phone, she said, "We need help."

Jay picked up the phone, his expression thoughtful.

"I know where she is, but I don't know who to trust at this point," he finally said out loud. "James, but I'm sure they're headed to Breezewood and he doesn't have any authority across state lines." Bitterness twisted Jay's expression. "I can't risk trusting the feds after Mitch betrayed us."

Kit plucked her phone back out of his hands. "Then we trust the people mom trusted," she said, while dialing.

The phone rang once and a voice answered, "Kit? What's going on? Where's your mom?"

"They took her, Aunt Mal. We need help."

Fourteen

Trixie

I was grateful that Butch didn't try to make small talk on the trip to Breezewood. I stared out the tinted window of the SUV, watching the miles fly by as they headed west, then north. My brain struggled to focus on planning for the upcoming meeting. I needed to be processing, considering options. But instead my mind's eye kept replaying the same moments over and over again.

I grasped the door handle and turned toward Jay. I was watching the sunlight from the open door track across his face when his eyes closed. It was as if someone pulled on a lasso around his waist, drawing him backwards and away from me.

Back in the car, I closed my eyes, keeping my breathing slow and steady and concentrated on keeping my face relaxed. Inside I wanted to scream and thrash but I held onto my control with an iron fist. To help Jay and Kit I had to get through the next hour alive. That was all that mattered right now. It was time to compartmentalize and focus.

As I finished my internal pep talk, the SUV pulled off of the highway and took a narrow road into the rolling hills. Butch spoke softly into his phone as we approached a black iron gate and it slid open smoothly to allow the two SUVs inside.

The driveway snaked around another hill and a stereotypical suburban McMansion sat in front of them, like a fat cat dressed in a frilly dress by a bratty child.

It was truly hideous.

Columns stood in a half circle around the two level entry-way, soaring from the stamped concrete pad to the convoluted roofline. The roof peaked in the middle as it arched out to meet the columns, the squat point flanked on each side with oddly arched eyebrow dormers. The windows in the dormers were square, leaving gaps around the casings, but the windows below those were arched at the tops. Only the bottom panes had mullions.

I got out of the SUV in a daze, standing and staring in horror at the monstrosity before me.

"Your uncle's pride and joy," Butch said, appearing beside me. "He designed it himself."

I whipped my head around to search his face for a trace of sarcasm and found none. Snapping my jaw shut, I smoothed out my face with a great deal of effort.

Butch looked at me expectantly, perhaps disappointed by my blank stare in the face of such magnificence. After a moment he gave up and waved me forward. I noted the two goons in front of the house and added them to the three who had traveled with us.

The inside of the house was as bad as the exterior, to my horror, and I was silently grateful for the distraction. I couldn't afford to get lost in thoughts of what might be happening elsewhere right now. The off-centered pattern of the parquet floor was the train wreck I needed to get my mind focused on the immediate issues at hand.

Following Butch up the marble staircase that curved through the large foyer, I found myself walking down a red berber carpet lined hallway, one of the new guys at my back. Butch paused at an open door and waved me through. I stepped into a dark paneled office and the large muscled man behind me followed, but Butch remained in the hall and pulled the door shut behind us. I strained to hear his footsteps in the hallway but the silence echoed. Either Butch was standing guard at the door or the room was soundproofed.

I turned slowly to the man sitting behind the desk. I'd put off looking directly at Cal for as long as I could. Given the circumstances under which we'd last seen each other, I had expected him to look much worse.

The right side of Uncle Cal's face was red and puckered, the eyebrow missing. But the eye looked fine, still a match for the other side, and the lips twisted slightly down but judging by the scowl aimed in my direction, they worked fine as well. The worst feature was the bare scalp on the right side, which arched back over his ear and revealed red and thickened patches of skin that stood out starkly against the thick white hair on the other side of his head. *Really, he should have just shaved the whole thing.*

"Looking a little rough there, Uncle Cal." I met those angry eyes and smirked.

There was a quick intake of breath from the goon behind me and I wondered if it was humor or horror, but then my attention was commanded by the spectacular meltdown before me.

"You bitch!" Cal screamed, launching to his feet. The previous pink cast over the scarred areas of his face was swamped by the color that poured up from his neckline. His entire face was now lobster red and spittle was forming at the corners of his mouth. "This is all your fault! You should have stayed gone!"

"Well, I have been trying," I pointed out calmly.

"It is fucking unbelievable the amount of trouble you have caused me," Cal flung at me, "for decades! Fucking DECADES!" Cal was up and out of his chair surprisingly quickly for a man in his 70s. He was thin and his shoulders didn't seem quite as wide as they once did, but Cal was still a big man. Even more intimidating, however, was the glock in his hand.

As he rounded his big wood desk, I tried to take a step forward and found myself anchored in place as beefy arms wrapped themselves around my chest.

"No more fucking around, Trixie," Cal yelled as he closed the distance between us, raising the gun in my direction and preparing to fire.

The guy behind me must have had the same thought that I did and decided he didn't want to be standing right behind me if Cal was about to start shooting. The arms across my chest dropped away and a large meaty hand wrapped around my left upper arm as the goon moved his body to the side.

I used my newfound freedom to spin backwards using my capture's grip as a pivot point as a gunshot rang from Cal's weapon. My momentum swung me behind the goon and pulled him into the spot where I'd been standing a split second earlier. Standing back to back now, I felt his body shudder with the impact of the bullet and the hand slipped from my arm. I was free and facing the door, but as I took a step forward, it swung open to reveal Butch, a gun in his hand.

Butch stood still, his face drawn as he took in the scene behind me. There was a thud as the guy who'd been my unwitting shield fell to the floor. I sidestepped away from the body, holding my arms up. Cal was still sputtering beside the desk.

"God damn it, Mikey!" Cal screamed at the man on the floor. His face edging from red into purple, Cal stomped over and began kicking him. Mikey flopped over onto his back and groaned, but Cal kept kicking at him.

"Boss! Boss, he's alive! What are you doing?" Butch snapped to life, waving the hand without the gun in Cal's direction. Butch moved closer to Mikey and I moved further to the side, waiting for a break in his focus.

"Stop it, Boss! You're killing him!" Butch was now standing over Mikey, opposite Cal, and was reaching out to grab the older man's arm.

"Get the hell off of me. She did this! It's all her fault," Cal cried, pointing his gun in my direction and firing wildly. I dived toward the door, counting on Butch to distract Cal enough for me to get away. Of course, chances were Cal would end up shooting him too, but at this point that wasn't my problem.

I made it to the top of the stairs only to find two more goons waiting for me halfway up the staircase. I hesitated and Butch came up behind me, grabbing my arm.

"Cal shot Mikey," Butch told the other two men, who exchanged a look. "He's still alive, but he's going to need a doctor."

"There's a lady doctor at the gate," one of the guys said.

"An animal doctor," the other corrected. "She got all turned around trying to make a house call. We were giving her directions when we heard the shot."

"Close enough," Butch replied. "Go get her."

Heart in my mouth, I watched one of the goons rush back down the stairs while the other continued up toward the landing where Butch and I stood. Butch pulled me around and marched me back toward Cal's office.

"He's crazy, you know," I said quietly. Butch glanced at me but didn't reply.

Back in the office, Cal had resumed his seat behind his desk, his head in his hands. When he glanced up at our entrance, the rage had faded from his face, along with it most of the color. The scars were still pink, but the surrounding skin was bone white. His lips twisted when he met my gaze.

"Help me put Mikey up on the sofa here," Butch directed the other man.

Ignoring them, Cal stared at me, his rage building again.

"This is all your fault, you little bitch," Cal seethed.

"How is any of this my fault, Uncle Cal?" I asked calmly.

"Just like that goddamn fire. Just like Jimmy," he continued, as if I hadn't spoken.

"Jimmy?" I asked, frozen. "My dad?" I held myself very still, not wanting to ask the next question. "What about Jimmy?"

"I just do what needs to be done," shouted Cal, his calmness deserting him again. He slammed a hand down on the desk, making everyone in the room jump. "For the family! I'm the only one who's looking out for the family, you selfish bastards."

"What did you have to do to Jimmy?" I asked carefully, glancing over at Butch, to see if he was following this. He and the other guy had gotten Mikey onto the couch and were sharing a look over his unconscious body.

"What did you do to Jimmy and Maureen, Uncle Cal?" I prompted again. I wasn't sure if Cal even knew who I was at that point.

"What I had to do," Cal repeated, more calmly. "No one walks. No one *retires*," he spit out in disgust.

"Is that what they wanted to do? Retire?" I asked, my heart breaking. If my parents had decided to retire, to walk away from the family business...There wasn't a doubt in my mind that they'd done that for me. And now I knew that Cal had killed them for it.

Suddenly, my mind felt laser focused. Cal had four henchmen standing, plus Butch. Shooting Mikey had not gone over well with Butch.

I was judging my chances of making a run at Cal when the door opened again, admitting the last person I expected to see and putting an end to my plan. You could only sacrifice yourself to risk taking out the bad guy when you knew you had a solid backup plan for your only child. When that backup plan walked into the room, it was time to go back to the drawing board.

Keeping my face blank, I turned away from the sight of my best friend walking into the room and kept my eyes on Cal.

"Who the fuck is this?" he said shortly.

"This is the doctor who stopped at the gate to ask directions," his guy answered. "She's going to look at Mikey."

"I'm not a physician," Mallory said. "I tried to tell him...I'm a veterinarian." She gestured at her house call bag slung over her shoulder. "But I'm willing to try to help while you wait for the ambulance." Mallory made a beeline for Mikey on the couch, not glancing in my direction as she crossed the room.

"Ambulance?" Cal asked. "Who called a fucking ambu-lance?" Butch walked over to Cal and spoke to him quietly while Mallory began unpacking supplies from her bag. I made sure no one's attention was on me before glancing at her quickly. She looked up and met my eyes, winking like a fruitcake. *I'll strangle her later*, I thought, looking back toward the quiet conversation taking place at the desk. *If we survive this.*

An old-fashioned ringtone sounded through the room and Butch pulled his phone from his pocket.

"It's Joey at the front gate," he said, answering the call on speaker. "What's up?" he asked, sounding braced for more bad news.

"There's a fucking school bus full of kids down here. They're looking for some high school I've never heard of and won't fucking leave. What do I do, man?" The tinny voice over the speaker was thick with panic. Butch walked over to the window and angled his head to try to get a view of the gate but I doubted he'd be able to see it from here.

"Get rid of them, Joey," Butch said shortly. "We've got enough on our hands at the moment." Ending the call, Butch walked over to the end of the couch and looked down at Mikey. "Will he make it?" Butch asked Mal, without looking at her.

"If we can stop the bleeding, he has a good chance," Mal told him in her smooth "I am a professional" voice. "I need to seal the wound and this will hurt. Can you hold down his feet? And I'll need someone else to hold down his shoulders," she said calmly, looking down at her tools.

Butch glanced up at the other goon still in the room, standing with his arms crossed by the door, and then looked over at me. I blinked back at him innocently.

"Trixie," he said, "you do it."

Cal made a noise from his place behind the desk and Butch whipped around at him. "Would you rather do it?" he asked aggressively and the tension in the room spiked.

Cal glanced over at the guy by the door and I could see the wheels spinning. Finally he shrugged and waved a hand in my direction, spinning his chair to stare sullenly out the window.

Butch nodded at me, "Trixie," he said calmly. I walked over and stood opposite him at the other end of the couch, Mikey's body between us and Mal kneeling beside him. Mal had opened Mikey's shirt and revealed a nasty hole in his side, slowly seeping blood onto Cal's couch.

Mal lifted a syringe and placed it beside the wound and looked up at me. "Ready?" she asked.

"No," I said firmly. I was not trying anything with her here.

Mal ignored me and began depressing the plunger on the syringe. Mikey's body jolted and Butch leaned over the arm of the couch on his end to press Mikey's feet back down to the couch as the man began to cry out. His eyes popped open as I pushed on his shoulders to keep him from sitting up and I felt something land on my foot.

Without looking down, I moved to a kneeling position as if I were trying to get better leverage against Mikey. The object Mal had placed on my foot ended up squeezed between my knees and it took a great deal of effort to not glance at the goon by the door.

Mal slapped a bandage over the wound and sat back on her heels.

"That's all I can do," she sighed, zipping up her bag. "I'd offer to wait with him until the ambulance arrives but I really do need to get to my appointment." Mal stood and looked at Butch expectantly.

He glanced at Cal, who didn't move from his glaring at the window. Butch waffled for a moment, then sighed.

"Tommy," he said to the goon by the door, "please escort the doctor back to her car." He turned to Mal, offering his hand. "Thank you for your help."

"You're very welcome," Mal responded, smiling.

As Mal and Tommy shuffled out the door, I placed one hand down to push myself off the floor, pocketing the object between my knees as I stood. Tommy closed the door behind him and Butch swung his attention back to me, pulling a gun from under his jacket.

"Did you help Cal kill my parents, Butch?" I asked calmly.

Butch glanced at Cal, who had finally turned his chair back to the room. Cal sat with his elbows on his desk, fingers laced before him, and looked at us both cooly.

"Butch!" I said sharply, pulling his eyes back to me. "Did you help Cal kill my parents?" I enunciated each word clearly. I needed to know.

"I didn't have anything to do with that, Trixie. I loved Jimmy and Maureen." Butch looked back at Cal. "Everyone loved Jimmy and Maureen."

"Is that right, Uncle Cal?" I asked. "Did you love your brother?"

Cal swung his cool, bland gaze toward me. He reached one hand under the desk and came back up with his gun.

"I've had enough of this shit," he said calmly. "I'm not going to let some stupid girl ruin this family."

"Girl? *Girl?*" I asked, arms akimbo. "I'm 40 years old, you dumbass."

"You dress like a fucking teenager. You're a disgrace to this family!" Cal accused, face starting to heat up again.

"You murdered your own brother, you piece of shit!" I screamed back at him.

Butch stood between us, looking increasingly uncomfortable. His gun had started to waver and was moving in Cal's direction. I wasn't the only one who noticed.

"Shoot her," Cal demanded abruptly and I could see Butch freeze, his face pale.

"Boss, let's think this through—" Butch started.

Cal raised his gun and fired, still seated at the desk. My whole body jolted and it took a moment for me to realize that I wasn't shot.

It was Butch sliding to the floor, red blossoming across his white shirt.

I pulled Mal's gun from my pocket and dived behind the sofa as the door to the office burst open. Pulling my legs in behind me, I swung around onto my knees expecting to see more of Cal's goons spilling into the room. I couldn't have been more shocked to see Jay standing there, a gun trained on Cal.

Fifteen

Trixie

The world stopped spinning for a moment. My eyes were locked onto Jay's face, taking in every detail, as I felt all of the blood rush from my head to my feet. It would have felt lovely to let myself collapse at that moment like a Victorian maiden and sag onto the couch, but we still had one issue left to resolve. And there was already a guy bleeding out on the couch. Time, sadly, resumed.

"Who the fuck are you?" Cal yelled, firing wildly towards Jay, who ducked back behind the door frame.

I popped over the arm of the couch and fired over Mikey's body. The bullet caught Cal in the meat of his shoulder and flung him back in his chair.

I bolted out of my cover and ran toward the door, crashing into Jay and letting the warmth of his body soak into mine for a second before grabbing his arm and heading for the stairs.

My elation crashed to a halt as we skidded to a stop at the top of the stairs. There were at least six more muscular armed henchmen heading up the curved staircase. I began wheeling backwards, pushing Jay behind me, when a deep voice rang out.

"Trixie!"

Memories began flooding through my head as I struggled to process what I was seeing. A tall, thin man, leaning heavily on a cane, stood at the bottom of the staircase. My memories overlaid what my eyes were seeing, trying to reconcile the booming voice of my grandfather to the frail old man before me.

"Grandpa?" I asked faintly. I felt Jay stiffen behind me and the two of us stood frozen as the wave of new goons flooded up the stairs and past us, into Cal's office. Two stood sentry at the top of the stairs as my grandfather walked between them. One of the men who had entered the office reappeared beside my grandfather to whisper into his ear.

Eying me and Jay, Grandpa waved an arm toward the office. Goons appeared on either side of us and plucked the weapons from our hands then firmly ushered us back into the room.

Cal was still sitting behind his desk, hand wrapped over his bleeding shoulder, his face pale. Butch was lying on the floor clutching his chest, his eyes open and sweat beaded on his forehead. Mikey was passed out on the couch or possibly dead at this point. I felt like it had been a while since anyone checked on him.

Jay and I were ushered to the right side of the room, opposite Cal's desk. He showed no reaction to our reappearance and sat in silence as we were followed into the room by four of the new men. He didn't react when my grandfather entered behind them. He was, however, caught by surprise when one of my grandfather's guards stepped toward the desk and snatched his gun from the surface. Cal fisted his hand and his jaw clenched as if he were gritting his teeth.

"Is Mikey dead?" my grandfather asked the room in general. I resisted the urge to respond to that deep voice and held my ground, still holding onto Jay's arm.

One of Grandpa's guards walked over to the couch and bent over Mikey for a moment. He rose and said, "He's alive. Doesn't smell like a gut shot, so he'll probably live." The guard stepped over to Butch and crouched on the ground beside him. "How you doing, man?"

"Not good," Butch answered. "But I think I'll live too." The guard nodded and got back to his feet, moving to stand at Grandpa's shoulder.

"Cal shoot you?" Grandpa asked shortly. Looking down at Butch, his face set.

"Yes, sir," Butch replied from his place on the floor. His throat worked for a moment, then he continued. "And Cal admitted to killing Jimmy and Maureen."

I was watching my grandfather's face and saw his eyes close for a moment.

"You suspected," I said quietly.

Grandpa opened his eyes and looked at me for a long moment. His eyes searching.

"You look like your grandmother, Trixie," he said finally.

"It's the hair," I pointed out. "My daughter has it too." It was a calculated risk to remind him of Kit's existence. Of course, that also reminded him of Jay, and Grandpa's eyes moved over to him, raking him up and down.

"This your man?" he asked.

"Yes," I replied firmly. Jay placed his hand over mine where it still clutched to his arm and our bodies moved a little closer together.

It was time to bring the conversation back on track.

"Did you know Cal killed my parents?" I asked him, pulling his focus back to me. The corners of my eyes stung and I clenched my jaw.

"Not at the time," he replied, sighing. His frame was thin but tall and straight despite the cane. He sagged a little and I could see him shift more weight onto the cane. "It has become harder and harder over the years to ignore the truth."

"The truth?" I echoed.

Grandpa sighed again and finally looked over at Cal, his face drawn down into a frown. "That my son is rotten. Bad to the core."

He moved his gaze back to me, nailing me with a firm glare. "I know what you think of the family business. I know it's what drove you away. But we are not bad people, Trixie. Your parents were not bad people."

"I know that!" I protested. "I loved my parents." I said more softly.

"And they loved you," Grandpa said, his face softening. "They knew how you felt and that our way of doing business had driven a wedge between you. Jimmy came to me and told me he was retiring."

"He did?" I lost the fight against the tears and they ran unchecked down my face.

"He and your mother were selling the house. They were going to buy a place out west, near your fancy school."

Now I was sobbing and Jay wrapped his arms around me, pulling me into his shoulder. My eyes were still glued to my grandfather's face and I realized I was shaking my head in denial when he nodded.

"It's true," he said. "Your parents loved you more than any-thing. They couldn't stand not having you in their lives." I could see the glisten of tears in Grandpa's eyes, but they didn't fall.

"Jimmy came to me and explained how they felt, that it was tearing them apart. He told me how well you were doing in school and how proud he was of you." Grandpa's eyes cut over to Cal and his lips firmed. "Cal was there. Jimmy told us he was retiring and Cal hit the roof."

"No one fucking *retires*," Cal spit out. His voice was low and vicious. His rage from that meeting had festered for over 20 years. "Jimmy was weak. I did what had to be done."

"You killed your brother," Grandpa said flatly.

"He was a traitor to the family!" Cal screamed, banging on his desk.

"Jimmy was the family," Grandpa said firmly. "And so was Maureen."

He turned to me. "And so is Trixie."

We weren't completely out of the woods but it seemed much less likely we were about to be shot.

Grandpa turned to one of his guards and gestured toward us with his chin. "Get them out of here."

The guard opened the door and looked at me expectantly. I hesitated. There were so many things I wanted to say but I had no idea where to start.

"I'm sorry," I said finally.

Grandpa's face softened, almost into a smile, and he shook his head. "You didn't do anything wrong, Trixie. None of this was your fault." Then his face hardened again. "You go now, Trixie. I'm going to take care of this and it's best if you and your man aren't here."

I nodded and crossed the room to the door without even a glance in Cal's direction, Jay close behind me.

As I passed through the doorway, Grandpa whispered, "Good luck, baby."

I glanced back but the guard was already pulling the door shut behind us. Wiping the tears from my face, I led the way down the hall, Jay on my heels.

Halfway down the stairs a shot rang out from above us.

Within seconds we were back outside. A part of me was surprised to see the sun still shining. So much had happened, how could it be the same day?

The guard unlocked a black SUV sitting in front of the house with a beep. "I'll take you guys into town and you can catch a ride from there, okay?"

"That would be great, thank you," I replied politely, sliding into the back seat. I caught Jay's glance my way as he followed me into the car, but he didn't say anything.

We sat in silence, still holding hands, as the car snaked down the long drive and cleared the electric gates. Turning back onto the main road, I could see a school bus parked on the side of the road up ahead.

Jay leaned forward and said, "You can leave us right here." The driver shrugged and pulled the car behind the bus. Jay swung open the door, pulling me out behind him.

"Thanks for the ride," I said.

A second later the car did a u-turn across the road and was headed back in the direction we'd come. I turned to Jay, hands on my hips.

"And just what exactly is a Fairfax County, Virginia school bus doing in Breezewood, Pennsylvania?" I asked, a brow arched. Jay's face split into a huge smile as the school bus door opened and people began pouring out. Mal, Diane, Doug, and a horde of teenage boys in football uniforms. And Kit and Char wearing cheerleader costumes. Was that Detective James in a Fairfax coach jacket?

My eyes threatened to spill over again and I spun and flung myself at Jay. I caught him by surprise and he shuffled a little on his feet, but his arms came around me immediately and I soaked in the warmth of his body. I felt Kit worm her way under his arm and tuck herself against me.

We ended up following the bus in Mal's car, which had been hidden behind it. Jay and I sat in the back with Kit beside me. Char was in the front next to her mom and spent the entire trip home backward in her seat, chatting excitedly with Kit.

Mal wanted to know every detail of every moment that she'd missed and I obliged. There were definitely some things I wish Kit didn't have to know, but after everything we'd been through there was no way I was keeping secrets from her.

I didn't even try to hold back my tears when I told her about her grandparents and what they'd been planning. It helped that Jay held my hand through it all.

***

I was standing at the kitchen counter the next evening when the doorbell rang. Kit sounded like a buffalo crossing the prairie as she ran to answer it.

My heart was in my throat as I rushed from the room, but paused in the kitchen doorway and bit my tongue as I watched her check who was there and then squeal with delight as she flung open the door. I wasn't sure if her excitement was for Jay or the two large pizzas he was holding, but she did kiss his cheek before grabbing the boxes from his hands and skipping past me into the kitchen.

Jay didn't mind being the victim of a teenage hit and run, judging by the broad smile on his face. He stepped into the house and shut the door behind him, dropping the duffle bag over his shoulder onto the floor by the stairs. We met in the middle of the room and I sank into the warmth of his chest, grabbing his face with both hands and kissing the hell out of him.

He hadn't been gone long, but the last few days had made me a little clingy. The only thing that could tempt me out of his arms was the heavenly aroma of cheese and pepperoni wafting in my daughter's wake.

Laughing, we pulled apart and followed Kit into the kitchen where she was already lifting a gooey slice free from the box now sitting on the table.

"That is a lot of cheese," I said, impressed.

"I received very clear instructions," Jay said, winking at Kit, who sighed happily as she bit into her slice.

"I missed this conversation," I noted, pulling my own piece onto a plate.

"We were talking on the bus on the way up to Breezewood yesterday," Jay explained.

I raised my eyebrows. "What else did you guys talk about?"

"So many things..." Jay taunted while Kit giggled suspiciously.

"Oh, great. Now you guys are going to conspire against me? Lovely," I rolled my eyes, and then completely ruined it by smiling like a loon.

The doorbell rang again and Jay and I shared a look as I got up from the table. At the door I turned back to find him standing in the doorway and waved him away. He gave me a confused look and I told him shortly, "I'm pretty sure there's never going to be a time when the idea of answering the door with you standing behind me doesn't fill me with anxiety. Go back in the kitchen or stand behind the door."

I gave him credit that he didn't roll his eyes at me and I was relieved when he moved to stand behind the door. I checked the peephole. "It's the detective," I said in surprise, swinging open the door.

Jay moved behind me and we both looked at Detective John James with a little trepidation. He'd been great yesterday and we'd both really appreciated his off-the-books help, but we weren't expecting him and couldn't help but wonder what was going on now.

"Everything okay, John?" Jay asked from my shoulder.

"Everything is fine. I just wanted to give you guys an update and I thought I'd stop by on my way home. If you're busy I can give you a call tomorrow morning instead..." his voice trailed off and he stepped back as if to make a break for it. Jay and I both started talking at once, reaching forward to draw him in.

"No, no, this is fine! Please come in."

"You're fine! Come on in! Do you like pizza?"

We herded the detective into the kitchen between us and had him sitting at the table and eating a gooey slice of mostly cheese in minutes. The four of us had demolished the first pizza and started on the second when he sat back and wiped his hands on a napkin. "Thanks, guys. That hit the spot."

"Long day?" I asked.

He nodded. "Jay's friends at the FBI have taken over the case. They picked up our buddy Issac last night and this morning they raided the house in Breezewood. There's no easy way to say this..." He hesitated for a moment. "They found Cal Bigotti dead of what appears to be a self-inflicted gunshot wound to the head."

"That's a shock," I said in a nearly believable tone. James rolled his eyes at me.

"Yeah, I'm sure it is," he replied in an equally sincere voice. "The good news is that he left a note confessing to a whole bunch of stuff that will keep the feds busy for quite some time."

I did raise my eyebrows a bit at that, but I suppose Grandpa would have found it expedient to have a handy scapegoat.

"I also spoke to the DA today," James continued. "Our surviving bank robber has accepted a plea deal." I gave him a fairly blank look. "That means no trial." I wasn't following. "That means we don't have to worry if we're calling Anne or Trixie to the stand."

"Ahhh," I said. "Yes, I can see how that will make life a little easier for everyone involved."

"Indeed," replied the detective. Finishing his water, he pushed back from the table and we followed suit. "Thank you both for the dinner. Time for me to head home."

Jay and I walked the detective out of the kitchen. I opened the door as Jay shook his hand. James turned to me, an eyebrow lifted.

"For the record," he said, "which one would it be?"

"Which one?" I asked, not following.

"Anne or Trixie?"

Ohhhh.

I looked over at Jay and he shrugged and smiled, no help. I knew he was okay with whatever I decided. Kit came to the kitchen doorway and leaned against the opening.

"Trixie is really growing on me," she said with a smile.

I shook my head and turned back to James with a shrug, smiling. The detective stuck out his hand and I shook it.

"Nice to meet you, Trixie," he said with a smile and a wink. "Try to stay out of trouble."

The three of us stood in the doorway and watched James get into his car and disappear around the corner. Jay's arm was wrapped around my shoulder and Kit came over and leaned against my other side. Night was beginning to fall and the streetlight in front of the house flickered to life. I closed the door and looked at my family.

"More pizza?"

About the Author

Mary Jane Owen is a pseudonym of Michael Owens, whose parents shouldn't be allowed to name things. Michael is a single mom, dog rescuer, teacher, and artist. She lives by the sea with her beautiful daughter and a rather large assortment of astonishingly lazy dogs.

For more works by Michael and the other amazing authors of Pepperback Press, please visit our website at PepperbackPress.com.